Hummingbirds *Fly* Backwards

Hummingbirds *Fly* Backwards

AMY CHEUNG

Translated by Bonnie Huie

amazon crossing

This is a work of fiction. Names, characters, organizations, places, events, and incidents are either products of the author's imagination or are used fictitiously.

Previously published as 三个A Cup 的女人 (*Three Women with A-Cup*) in 2008 by Beijing October Arts & Literature Publishing House and 我这辈子有过你 (*You Are Everything to Me*) in 2014 by Hunan Literature & Art Publishing House in Mainland China. Translated from Chinese by Bonnie Huie.

Published by AmazonCrossing, Seattle

www.apub.com

ISBN-13: 9781503935976
ISBN-10: 1503935973

Cover design by David Drummond

Printed in the United States of America

1

Women and Their Bras

Hong Kong, 1995

I've always wanted to write a story whose protagonist was a bra. The bra could narrate the more than century-long history of its own evolution. In the old days, Chinese women wore a full-frontal undergarment called a *dudou.* Bras, however, are a product derived from the West. In the nineteenth century, young women from wealthy families wore corsets made from canvas, whalebone, wire, and lace. The corsets were designed to shape a woman's body into an hourglass figure, but over time they damaged the internal organs of the women who wore them. In 1889, a corset maker in Paris by the name of Herminie Cadolle invented the world's first brassiere: an article of clothing that could be fastened across the chest and yet wouldn't constrict the diaphragm's movements.

Though it didn't necessarily confine the abdomen, a bra was a complete monstrosity. In 1913, a debutante named Caresse Crosby asked her personal maid to sew two handkerchiefs together to make a simple bra, using pink silk ribbons for the shoulder straps. In 1935, the undergarment maker Warner's invented the bra cup, whose sizes ranged from an A to a D. The 1960s saw a bra-burning revolution. In the '90s, fashion designers made bras that could be worn as outer garments, and bras were back in vogue again. Breast enlargements soon became the second most popular type of cosmetic surgery. Women and their bras.

My first bra wasn't my own. It was my mother's. One day, my mother said, "Chow Jeoi, it's time you started wearing a bra." Since I didn't have the courage to buy my own, I secretly wore my mother's. That bra was beige, with a daisy between the cups. I bought my first bra from a street vendor who was pushing a handcart heaped with dozens of bras through the city center. It was truly a sight to behold.

Today I work as the manager of an intimate apparel boutique that specializes in luxury brands of French and Italian lingerie. If my recent experiences have taught me anything, it's that, for women, love and intimate apparel are inseparable.

The boutique is on the second floor of a shopping center, amid a veritable gold mine of upscale shops in the heart of Central, which is Hong Kong's financial district. The shop has two other employees: Anna, who's twenty-six, and Jenny, who's thirty-eight. Anna is one seriously hardworking young woman, but she's always getting sick. She gets bad menstrual cramps, and her complexion is pale year-round. Jenny, a mother of two, is a brilliant PR-type who really knows how to connect with customers. She's tough as nails, and she and Anna make a great team. Anna weighs about 90 pounds and Jenny well over 130, so there's no way that our typical customer would ever compare herself and feel bad.

There's one main guiding principle when it comes to luxury bras: the less it covers, the more expensive it is. Lack of coverage equals sexy, and achieving sexiness without vulgarity is an art form. If a woman can make a man think she's sexy without finding her vulgar, then the bra did its job.

Smart women understand that sexiness is an investment. That's why we have no shortage of customers—even with the hefty price tags.

Our customers consist primarily of high-income career women. Rich housewives aren't willing to spend that kind of money. I saw the bra of a rich housewife once. It was worn to tatters, and the underwire was even sticking out. When a woman gets married, it's all too easy for her to assume that everything is perfectly settled, so there's no need to worry about lingerie anymore. The biggest enemy of the lingerie business isn't the economic climate—it's marriage. What is good for business, though, are extramarital affairs.

One day, we were just about to close when my friend Chui Yuk popped in. I saw several men give her the once-over as they passed by the store. She was a fetching 36B.

"Chow Jeoi, do you have a pencil?" Chui Yuk asked me.

"How about a pen?" I said as I handed her one.

"No, I need a pencil."

As I dug a pencil out of a drawer, I asked, "What are you writing?"

"I just wrapped up a swimsuit shoot. The director told me I should put a pencil under one of my breasts. If the pencil stays put, that means it's sagging."

I'd met Chui Yuk by chance three years earlier. I was working in a design department at the time, and Chui Yuk had responded to a call for fitting models. I noticed her right away. She has an amazing figure—five foot eight and 36-24-36—with a pale complexion and long, slender legs, which made her absolutely picture-perfect for lingerie. From the moment we met, we were practically inseparable, and we've been the best of friends ever since. Once, there were some bras that I'd put my heart and soul into designing. I'd pitched the concepts to my boss in France, in the hopes that he would recommend them to the higher-ups. He wasn't interested. When Chui Yuk heard about it, she invited my boss out to dinner and did everything in her power to put in a good word for me. In the end, he said he'd send my work on to the head office in France. Unfortunately, I never heard back from the head office.

"How's it going? Are you sagging?" I asked.

"Fortunately not," she said, sounding satisfied.

"Being well-endowed isn't necessarily a good thing," I warned her. "Heavy ones start sagging sooner."

"I don't think weight is what causes breasts to sag. And it's not gravity, either," Chui Yuk said.

"So what is it, then?"

"Men's hands," she said, giggling. "It's their hands. They just don't know how to be a little gentler." Chui handed the pencil back to me. "I want to buy a new bra."

"Didn't you just buy a new one last week?" I asked her.

"Don't remind me. A few days ago, I wasn't careful when I hung it out to dry, and it fell onto the awning below. Today I saw a bird using it to build a nest."

"That has to be the world's most expensive bird's nest," I said.

"That bird probably never expected to enjoy the luxury of a French-made lace nest right here in Hong Kong," said Chui Yuk with a wry laugh.

It was ten minutes past closing time. I told Jenny and Anna they could go home.

"Are you looking for something elegant?" I asked Chui Yuk.

"I'm looking for something that'll make a man's heart race," she said, sticking her chest out.

"Why not just get something that'll give him a heart attack!" I picked out a handmade white viscose and lace three-quarter-cup bra and gave it to her. Three-quarter cups were sexier than full cups, since they revealed more cleavage. The unusual feature of the one I chose was a colorful Mickey Mouse between the cups, for a touch of innocence within the sexiness.

"It's so cute," Chui Yuk remarked as she headed to the dressing room, and I went to lock up.

"Come look. It doesn't seem like it fits," Chui Yuk called, craning her head from inside the dressing room.

"Let's see." I took a peek.

She was staring into the mirror dejectedly.

"I look fat. That's what I learned at the swimsuit shoot."

The bra looked flawless. Her breasts were practically suffocating the Mickey Mouse between them.

"Lean over," I said.

As she leaned over, I helped her adjust herself so that her breasts filled the cups to the brim.

"That's how you put it on. It's not that it doesn't fit—you just need to get it in place."

"Is this how you always help people?" she asked.

"It's my job."

"I'm so glad you're not gay."

"Don't be silly! Just because someone's gay doesn't mean she's into your body type."

"I'll take this one, please, ma'am!"

"Got it."

"Oh my God," she suddenly squealed, "I forgot to buy the magazine!"

"What magazine?"

"*National Geographic*."

"You read *National Geographic*?"

"It's for Yu Mogwo. He needs it for a novel he's working on. But all the bookstores must be closed by now." Yu Mogwo was Chui Yuk's boyfriend. By day, he was an editor at a newspaper. By night, he was a budding science-fiction writer. Yu Mogwo was his pen name. His real name had a Yu in it, but I couldn't remember the rest of it.

Chui Yuk liked calling him Yu Mogwo around other people. She took pride in saying those three characters—*yu mo gwo*—and was firmly convinced that their meaning—"It was written in the stars"—would come to pass in the not-so-distant future. I thought Yu Mogwo was a pretty clever pen name. Similarly, my motto was "If the bra fits, wear it."

"Come with me to find a copy," she said, sounding anxious.

"Where are we going to find one this late? The bookstores and newsstands in Central are all closed by now."

"Maybe there's one that's still open. Let's go see."

"I have to lock up the shop. You go on ahead. There's a newsstand across from the New World Tower. Maybe someone's still there."

Chui Yuk darted outside in her three-inch heels.

When I walked up to the newsstand twenty minutes later, I found her sitting on a flight of stone steps, looking annoyed.

"It's closed." She pointed to the newsstand. All the magazines were locked up inside two giant wooden boxes.

"You can buy it tomorrow."

"The new issue came out today. I promised I'd bring it to him tonight."

"It's not like he's going to kill you for not bringing him a magazine."

Chui Yuk looked up, then shot me a meaningful glance. "Do you think there's a copy inside that wooden box?"

"You want to steal it?"

"It's not stealing." She crouched down to examine the crude locks on the box.

"I'll take the magazine and leave the money inside the box. I'm buying it fair and square!" Chui Yuk dumped out the contents of her handbag and rifled through them until she found a nail file. She started to pry open the lock on the box.

"Don't!"

"Shh!" she said, signaling for me to keep watch for her.

My heart was pounding wildly. I wasn't ready to get locked up in jail for stealing a copy of *National Geographic*. Chui Yuk was taking an awfully long time. I was sweating like crazy as she fiddled around.

"Let me try," I said, glancing over at her.

"What are you two doing?" a man wearing a security-guard uniform shouted from the top of the steps.

Chui Yuk scrambled to gather her belongings and took off running, pulling me behind her. We ran all the way to Statue Square. When the coast was finally clear, we stopped.

"So, you'd actually commit a crime for him. Is there anything you wouldn't do for him?"

"I'd do anything for him. I'd die for him," she said, gazing into the distance.

I burst out laughing.

"What's so funny?"

"I've never heard anyone say that in real life. Seriously, though, it's touching," I told her earnestly.

"Would you die for your man?"

"I don't know if he'd die for me."

"I have a feeling that Yu Mogwo is the last man I'm ever going to be with."

"You say that with every guy."

"This time it's different. Yu Mogwo and I have been together for two years now. This is the longest I've ever been in love. I truly admire him, and he's taught me so much. He's like an alien who's been catapulted into my world to show me what love and the meaning of life are."

"An alien? That sounds like something straight out of a science-fiction novel."

"I don't know. Yu Mogwo has a powerful imagination. It's nice to be with a man like that."

"With all this gushing, who needs imagination? How are you going to explain why you didn't buy him a copy of *National Geographic* today?"

"I got a bra."

"Will the bra make up for the *National Geographic*?"

"Of course not."

"So what difference does it make?"

"But . . ." She pulled the bra out of its bag, made a seductive face, and said, "All I need is to put on this bra. It's sure to drive him wild, and he'll forget all about this magazine business for tonight."

I'd met Yu Mogwo a few times. He was slim and quite handsome, and he liked to wear dress shirts and jeans with white socks and sneakers. He was in his thirties and not the least bit athletic. There's something a little rebellious about men who wear white socks and sneakers. It's like they just don't want to grow up. Although Yu Mogwo wasn't even close to tall, he was clearly a man of great stature in Chui Yuk's heart. Whenever Yu Mogwo spoke, Chui Yuk listened attentively. Yu Mogwo could be rather arrogant when he was around her. It made me realize that a man's arrogance stems from the adoration of the women around him.

Yu Mogwo and Chui Yuk had known each other for a month before they moved in together. Most science-fiction writers are generally assumed to be science or computer geeks, but Yu Mogwo was no science geek and hadn't a clue about computers. He was really going out on a limb.

Yu Mogwo had published a novel, but I didn't care much for science fiction and hadn't read it. It hadn't sold well, which Chui Yuk blamed on the publisher being too small, the publicity being inadequate, and the printing quality being subpar.

"Do you feel like going to a movie?"

"We've already watched all the X-rated movies that came out recently. Is there anything else worth seeing?"

"There's still one we haven't seen."

Watching X-rated movies had become a shared pastime ever since we'd gone to one the year before. X-rated movies were the ultimate form of comic entertainment; no bona fide comedy even came close. Those tough, muscular men and seductively silhouetted women didn't need a reason to strip naked and jump into bed. Chui Yuk and I always erupted into sidesplitting laughter in the theater.

The sight of two women going to see an X-rated movie together always drew puzzled stares from other people, but that was precisely what made it so much fun. It's an arena where men are expected to come parading in, looking for a little sensory stimulus. But for women, the atmosphere is more like that of a haunted house—a cheap thrill, and nothing more.

There were only a handful of people in the theater. Chui Yuk and I kicked back and put our feet up on the seats in front of us. We munched on handfuls of popcorn as we judged the bodies of the male and female leads.

"That guy's got some killer pecs," Chui Yuk said.

I snuggled up against Chui Yuk without saying a word.

"Did you two have another fight?' Chui Yuk asked.

"He won't fight with me," I said.

After exiting the theater, Chui Yuk and I parted ways. I went back to my place. I lived alone in a 650-square-foot apartment on the second floor of a six-story walk-up amid the bustling nightlife of the Lan Kwai Fong district. Below me, on the ground floor, was a specialty cake shop owned by a Chinese-Indonesian woman named Kwok. She was in her fifties and a little on the plump side. Born and raised in Indonesia, she spoke fluent Cantonese. She had a rather distinctive way of making cakes, namely in that she used frosting.

"Cakes with frosting are the most delicious kind," she had told me proudly.

The cakes she made were gorgeous. I once saw one that was turquoise. It was the most beautiful cake I'd ever seen in my life.

Her cake shop was never advertised. Her business largely came from custom orders. Word of mouth was good, and the customers kept trickling in. Every cake was personally made by Ms. Kwok. I inhaled the scent of those cakes when I woke up every morning. It was the added bonus of living in that apartment.

The cake shop normally closed at eight, but when I got home that night, I noticed Ms. Kwok was still there.

"Ms. Kwok, what are you doing here?"

"I'm waiting for a customer to pick up an order," she said.

"There are people who need cake at this hour?"

Just then, a middle-aged man walked into the shop.

Ms. Kwok handed the cake to him, and they left the shop together. Was it her husband? It couldn't be. She'd just said that it was a customer. Was it possible that the cake was merely a pretext to conceal the fact that she was having an illicit affair? The man was pretty good looking. Though Ms. Kwok was middle-aged, she had an ample bosom. I estimated she was a 36B.

I went up to my apartment, took off my shirt and pants, and turned on the faucet. Then I removed my bra. I didn't normally wash my undergarments as soon as I got home, but it was a particularly hot night, and Chui Yuk and I had sprinted a few hundred yards to get away from the guard. It was important to me to get my bra clean again since it was my very favorite. It was a pink memory-foam bra that molded itself to your figure if you wore it regularly, and it retained its shape even after several washings. I don't know if the idea came from those cars with driver recognition systems—where the seat automatically returns to its last position when the driver gets in and turns the key—but I think a memory-foam bra is much more practical.

The memory feature wasn't the main reason I loved this bra. I'd worn it during my first rendezvous with Tong Man Sam, and he'd gone so far as to compliment it. It made me feel like a woman whenever I wore it.

It was unlikely that Sam would call me that night.

I slept restlessly, right up to the moment when I woke to the scent of cake from downstairs. The sky was overcast, and it was drizzling. The bra I'd washed the night before wasn't completely dry, so I put on a white bra and a white dress. It wasn't ideal weather for wearing white, but I couldn't find any other dresses in my closet that weren't wrinkled.

As I headed out, I said good morning to Ms. Kwok as usual. She was in a chipper mood. She didn't seem the least bit affected by the bad weather—maybe she'd had a good time last night.

Sam was waiting for me outside. He wore a navy-blue suit and a white shirt. His collar was unbuttoned, and I saw that his tie was in his bag. He'd worked overnight.

"What are you doing here?" I asked him, deliberately trying to maintain my composure.

"I wanted to see you. Can we have breakfast?"

"Aren't you tired?"

"I'm used to it."

Seeing how haggard he looked after his shift, I didn't have the heart to refuse.

"I have some food at home."

Sam and I went upstairs to my place, and I called Jenny to tell her I'd be late.

I set down my handbag, put on an apron, and started making a ham sandwich in the kitchen.

Sam came into the kitchen and wrapped his arms around my waist.

"Do you know where I was last night?" I asked him.

He pressed his face into my hair.

"You never know where I was the night before." I choked back a sob.

"I trust you," Sam said.

"If I had died last night, you wouldn't have found out until this morning. If I had been with another man last night, you wouldn't have any idea."

"You would do that?"

"I hope I do," I said.

If I weren't so madly in love with this man, I'd probably be a little happier. Love is a kind of burden. Sam worked as a foreign exchange trader at a bank. We'd been together for four years, and I didn't know that he was already married when I first met him. But I kept seeing him all the same.

Four years ago, on the night he had taken me out to celebrate my twenty-fifth birthday, I finally asked him, "Are you married?"

He had gazed back at me with a pained expression, and I knew it meant he belonged to another woman.

Being caught in a love triangle, I had no choice but to believe in love more strongly than any other woman. If there were no such thing as love, I'd be nothing but a home-wrecker.

After finishing his ham sandwich, Sam splayed out on the sofa.

"Are you tired?" I asked.

He nodded.

I made him put his head on my lap and started massaging him. Then he clasped my hand and asked, "You don't hate me, do you?"

I remained silent. I'd never hated him. But he could only see me twice a week and never on Sundays. When I was still living with my family, I'd go meet him at a bar every week. After two years of doing that, I asked him one day, "Why don't we rent a place together? I don't want to meet up at a bar anymore. Doing it like this makes me feel like I'm a bad woman."

So Sam and I found the apartment I live in now. He paid my rent. I felt like he and I had finally settled down together, though in actuality, it wasn't our shared home. I painstakingly decorated the apartment, hoping that he'd move in.

Sam once told me that he had to leave me. "How often does a woman get to be twenty-five?" he'd asked. He didn't want me to squander my youth, and he clearly had no plans to marry me. But he'd come back to me not long after that. We had a huge fight about once a month. I couldn't accept the fact that he'd have sex with me, then get dressed and go back home. The thought of him sleeping next to another woman drove me mad. A couple of days earlier, we'd gotten into an argument because I wanted him to stay the night. Though I knew it was out of the question, I just couldn't help ask.

"Feel any better?"

He nodded.

"How is it that men can love two different women at the same time?"

"Maybe they're afraid of dying," Sam said.

I fondled his ears.

"You need to get to work. You're the manager, you know."

"Who can muster the energy to go to work in this kind of weather?" I sprawled out on the sofa.

Sam pulled me up.

"I'll take you to work."

"If you loved me, you'd indulge me," I said brazenly.

"That's no way to love you." He started dragging me out the door.

"I know there'll be a day when I'm alone, since you won't say when you're going to leave me."

"I'm never going to leave you," Sam said, taking my hand.

That's what he always said, but I never believed him. I figured we'd break up eventually.

***

Business was lousy that day, so I let Anna and Jenny go to lunch together. While they were out, a woman in her twenties came into the store. Judging by the way she was dressed and made up, I figured she probably worked in the neighborhood. She was incredibly curvaceous—a 34C, I guessed.

She picked out a black lace bra and girdle.

"Are you a 34C?" I asked her.

Looking surprised, she nodded. "How did you know?"

"Just a professional hunch," I said, smiling.

She was in the fitting room for a long time.

"How's that working out for you?" I called out to her.

"I'm not sure how to put on this girdle."

"Let me help you."

When I stepped into the fitting room, I discovered that the woman had four breasts. In addition to the usual two, she had two more breasts underneath. The extra breasts were only slight bulges—so small that they'd only need a double-A cup.

I practically shrank back in fear. But to avoid causing any embarrassment, I carried on as if nothing were out of the ordinary and helped her with the girdle.

"You have to take a deep breath when you put this on. Also, you have to fasten the front first, and then turn it around and do the back."

As I was helping her with it, my hand accidentally brushed against one of the smaller breasts.

"Do you think they're weird?" she suddenly asked me.

"Hmm?" I didn't know what to say.

"Don't be alarmed. They're natural. Science says that throughout the course of the human anatomy's evolution, there have been aberrations. I guess I haven't finished evolving."

"Are they a nuisance?" I asked her awkwardly.

"I'm used to them, so they're not much of a nuisance. My husband doesn't mind, either."

It hadn't occurred to me that this woman might be married. I would've guessed that having four breasts would be an obstacle to dating. I guess I was wrong—maybe four breasts meant double the pleasure. To wish for two breasts and get four instead might be like getting an added bonus.

"There is a downside," she said. "The risk of getting breast cancer is higher than average."

I would've thought she would be embarrassed about having four breasts—not treat it as a privilege. But she seemed perfectly happy to tell me all about them.

"Fortunately, these two don't hurt when I get my period," she said, cupping the two lower breasts.

I nodded and listened in amazement.

If a man had a wife with four breasts, would he still want a mistress? When a man loves more than one woman, is it because he wants four breasts?

Sam called before I left work, and I told him that I'd met a woman with four breasts.

"Did that really happen?"

"Would you ever want a woman with four breasts?"

"Doesn't sound so bad."

"Did you go in search of another woman because you wanted four breasts?"

"Hey, I already have two of my own. Including yours, that's four," he said. "I don't need to go out and get more."

"Since when do you have breasts? You only have nipples, silly," I said, laughing.

"Do you have class today?"

"I'm headed there now."

I had enrolled in a fashion design program, which was taught by a designer named Chen Dingleung. I'd read interviews with him in the paper, but I hadn't met him until I arrived at class.

He wore a simple navy-blue shirt and stonewashed jeans with loafers.

He wrote his full birthdate out on the blackboard. As it turned out, we had the same birthday.

"I'm a Scorpio—oozing with mystery, sex appeal, and passion. I also represent death. When this day comes, don't forget to give me a birthday present," Chen Dingleung said.

It was the first time I'd ever met a man who shared my birthday. I was delighted.

After class, I went to a bakery in a nearby department store. On the way, I passed a toy store that had a jigsaw puzzle that intrigued me. It showed a scene at a little restaurant in rural France. The restaurant was in a two-story building with an antiquated facade. The paint was peeling off the walls, and a cloud of cigarette smoke lingered near the ceiling. A couple who I imagined to be the restaurant's owners sat at one of the outdoor dining tables, leisurely drinking red wine. Sam liked to drink red wine and eat well, and I'd told him that if he could ever escape that job of his—which was slowly draining him of his youth—we should open a restaurant together. He'd be in charge of the wine and the kitchen, and I'd tend to the guests. Lonely customers would come by to drink and chat. Every time I mentioned this dream of mine, Sam would laugh and nod. I knew that it would never become a reality. But just longing for that distant image of perfection—in which it was just the two of us—made me a little happier.

I never imagined I'd find an exact replica of that restaurant. The only thing that was different was the location. Just as I was paying for the puzzle, a man hurried past me with a baguette tucked under his arm. It was Chen Dingleung. He paused when he saw me.

"Are you a fan of jigsaw puzzles?"

"It's the first time I've ever bought one."

"Are you a Scorpio? You seem a lot like me," he said.

"Really? Maybe so. My job's all about sex appeal. I work at a lingerie shop."

"What made you choose this one?" He pointed at the puzzle with the baguette.

"The restaurant is just so charming," I said.

"I've been there," he said.

"Really? Where is it?"

"It's in Cherbourg, France."

"Cherbourg?"

"It's a beautiful place. There's a French film called *The Umbrellas of Cherbourg* that was shot there. Do you know the song 'I Will Wait for You'? That's the theme."

Chen Dingleung started to rap the baguette on the counter to the beat of the music.

"You're probably too young to have seen the movie," he said.

"You seem pretty nostalgic about it," I said.

"Nostalgia is one of the dangers of middle age."

"Is this couple supposed to be the owners?"

Chen Dingleung studied the man and the woman in the puzzle.

"I don't know. I was in Cherbourg ten years ago. Was this puzzle expensive?"

"Very." I had paid more than two hundred Hong Kong dollars for it.

"Puzzles with people and scenery can be rather tricky, you know!"

"Good for killing time." I pointed to his baguette. "Is that your dinner?"

Chen Dingleung nodded. It was like he was waving a baton. We went our separate ways at the toy store, and I headed to the bakery, where I bought a baguette of my own.

As I exited the department store, it started pouring. With my baguette in hand, I was suddenly stuck. Chen Dingleung appeared again.

"Are you heading across the harbor?" he asked.

I nodded slightly.

"I'll give you a ride. Catching a cab can be a challenge in this weather."

"Is it hard to find that song, 'I Will Wait for You'?"

"It's such an old song that I don't know where you'd find it. Let me look into it. Lots of people have covered it."

"Thanks. What's *The Umbrellas of Cherbourg* about?"

"It's basically about a pair of young lovers who are destined to meet but not to stay together. They meet again at a gas station years later, when they're each married with kids."

Chen Dingleung pulled up to a gas station.

"Sorry. Just have to fill up the tank."

"You must have a really good memory if you can still remember it."

"When I saw it, it moved me. That's why I've remembered it all this time."

"Is it out on video?"

"It's such an old film that I don't think it'd be released on video. Good things should be left in your memory. If you see it again, you'll be in a different frame of mind and you might not like it anymore."

"Some things are timeless, though."

Chen Dingleung chuckled. "Like ill-fated love?"

"Yes."

I missed Sam.

Chen Dingleung pulled up to the entrance of my building.

"See you later," I told him.

As soon as I walked in I cleared off the dining-room table. I took out the box containing the jigsaw puzzle. I dumped out its contents and started sorting the pieces by color. I couldn't wait to put together the restaurant in the dream that Sam and I shared. The puzzle would be my birthday present to him.

The puzzle wasn't as easy to assemble as I'd imagined. It took me all night just to finish one edge.

In the morning, I was startled awake by the sound of the phone ringing. It was Sam. I'd fallen asleep slouched over the dining-room table.

"I found the restaurant we talked about!" I told him.

"Where is it?" Sam asked me.

"It's right in front of me. It's on a jigsaw puzzle. Do you want to see it?"

"I'll join you for lunch."

I was in a good mood when I arrived at the lingerie shop. Chui Yuk called to see if I wanted to have lunch.

"I can't today."

"Are you meeting Sam?"

"Uh-huh. What about Yu Mogwo?"

"He's busy working on his novel. He's already half done and trying to pick up the pace. I'm worried that I'll distract him if I hang out at the house. Besides, there's something I want to talk to you about."

"What happened?"

"My bras have been disappearing recently."

"Are more crows using them to build nests?"

"I've been making sure that the clothespins are super, super secure. I don't think a crow could make off with one. I can't imagine that someone has been stealing my bras."

"Unless that person is a pervert."

"That's one possibility."

"You'd better be careful!" I teased her.

***

At lunchtime, I went home and continued working on my puzzle until Sam arrived with takeout.

"Doesn't it look just like our restaurant?" I asked him.

"It's a dead ringer. I can't believe it actually exists," he said.

"Have you ever seen the movie *The Umbrellas of Cherbourg*?"

Sam shook his head.

"Have you ever heard the song 'I Will Wait for You'?"

"I seem to have some vague recollection of a song by that name."

Sam picked up a piece of the puzzle.

"Don't work on my puzzle!"

"I used to be able to finish a puzzle a week, though I don't think I've ever put together such an elaborate one."

"You were into puzzles? You never told me that before." I sat down in Sam's lap.

"It was back in college, when I had more free time. I put together dozens of them."

"Where are they now? You should give them to me."

"I have no idea what I did with them. Are you going to put this one together all on your own?"

"Uh-huh."

"You have the patience?" He looked at me, his eyes brimming with doubt.

"Free time is something I have loads of. I spend most of my time waiting for you."

"You know what the secret to solving puzzles is?"

"What's the secret?"

"Buy the easiest ones possible. This one is too complicated."

"I'm completely confident that I can finish this one. You just wait and see."

"What a wonderful smell! They must be baking cakes downstairs." Sam inhaled deeply.

"Do you want one? I'll go buy one." I stood up.

"No. I have to go to work. I'll take you back."

I ran my fingers through Sam's hair. "You're starting to go gray."

"Because I have to deal with you."

"Don't blame me. It's your super stressful job. Can't you cut back on your hours?"

"In a few years, no one's even going to want to hire me."

"You're not even forty yet." Suddenly, it dawned on me how child-like he was.

As Sam walked me back to the shop, I took his hand, but he quickly pulled it free. "Why don't you go the rest of the way? I'll talk to you later," he said and hurried off in the opposite direction. It wasn't the first time he'd ditched me out of the blue. He must've seen someone that he knew. I stared ahead at the faces in the crowd. Could his wife be among them?

I continued down the street in a daze. I was the other woman. That was the fate I'd been handed. I wiped away my tears before heading inside the store, where Chui Yuk was busy chatting with Jenny and Anna.

"You're back! I was just telling them all about the bra-snatching pervert," Chui Yuk said.

"What are you planning to do about your bra thief?" Anna asked.

"Ugh, if I could only catch him . . ."

"You should cover his head in a gunny sack and beat him up, then castrate him and parade him through town before having him drawn and quartered," I said.

"It's not that serious a crime, is it? It's not like he committed murder," said Chui Yuk, looking at me bewildered.

I was merely venting my frustration. The phone rang. I knew it was Sam even before I picked up.

"I saw her younger sister up ahead while we were walking."

"Oh, really? Did she see you?" I asked coldly.

He said nothing.

"I have to get back to work," I said and hung up the phone.

"We should try to catch that thief tonight!" I said, turning to Chui Yuk.

"Tonight?"

"You said he likes to come at night, didn't you?"

"But I don't know if he'll show up tonight. Besides, Yu Mogwo won't be home."

"We don't need a man's help with this kind of thing. Besides, men who steal underwear aren't the violent type."

After work, I headed to Chui Yuk's place with her.

"Do you have the bait ready?" I asked.

"Bait?"

"A bra! You need an especially enticing one."

Chui Yuk went into her bedroom and emerged a moment later with an elegant red lace bra.

"You have a red bra?" I was taken aback.

"It was an impulse buy that I made ages ago," she said, sounding embarrassed. "He likes stealing colorful bras. Everything except white. He'll definitely go for this one."

Chui Yuk hung the red bra out on her balcony.

We turned off all the lights in the house and stationed ourselves where we had a view of the balcony. The two of us had guessed that the thief was a neighbor who got to the second-floor balcony by shimmying up the storm drain along the side of the building.

I sat down in a chair and asked Chui Yuk, "Do you have any weapons?"

"Does a mop count?"

She ran into the kitchen and came back with a wet mop. "It's not dry yet."

"Let's not use that. Let's use a broom."

"Our mop is our broom."

"You use a mop to sweep? I can't imagine!"

"Oh! I know!" Chui Yuk said. "I'll use one of Yu Mogwo's belts!"

She picked up a men's leather belt off the sofa and waved it.

"A belt? I'm scared he might like it!"

"What should we do, then?"

"Don't you have a racket or anything like that?"

"I have a badminton racket."

"That'll do."

Chui Yuk and I sat and waited from ten o'clock until midnight, but there wasn't the slightest hint of activity around the balcony.

"Do you think he'll show up?" Chui Yuk asked. Suddenly, the phone rang. It made both of us jump.

Chui Yuk answered it.

"It's Yu Mogwo," she said.

I rested my head against the chair. If only Sam were here. I was feeling sort of scared.

Just then, a human silhouette appeared outside on the balcony.

"It's him. Hang up the phone," I whispered to Chui Yuk.

As the culprit snuck up to Chui Yuk's red bra and took hold of it, I stormed out onto the balcony. In the confusion, I took the chair with me and threw it at him. The chair missed, but Chui Yuk lifted her racket and whacked him. Then she grabbed a pile of random things that she threw at him. Completely bewildered, the culprit leapt to his feet and tumbled over the side of the balcony onto the first-floor awning. He rolled off and fell to the ground.

We sprinted downstairs. Several men had already apprehended the thief, who was still clutching the bra in one hand. Contrary to what I'd expected, he wasn't hideous at all. He had a fair complexion and a crew cut, and he looked to be in his thirties.

Someone called the police. When they arrived, Chui Yuk and I had to go to the station to file a report. The bra thief sat dejectedly in the corner.

I felt a slight tinge of regret. I hadn't foreseen that this would drag on into the wee hours of the night, or that this man could have fallen to his death—which would have made Chui Yuk and me guilty of manslaughter, though we could've claimed it was committed in self-defense. At the end of the day, a bra wasn't worth the price of anyone's life.

"Whose bra is this?" the male police officer on duty asked Chui Yuk and me.

"It's mine," Chui Yuk answered, looking a bit embarrassed.

"We're going to have to hold onto this as evidence."

"Evidence?" Chui Yuk and I looked at each other in dismay.

"This will serve as evidence in court that the suspect did in fact commit the crime."

"I don't want to press charges," said Chui Yuk.

"You don't want to press charges?" the police officer asked.

"That's right. Can I take this bra and go?"

The bra thief was so touched that he started to sob.

Chui Yuk and I left the police station together, and she tossed the bra into a trash can.

"Oh no! I just remembered!" Chui Yuk shrieked, turning pale. "Did I throw a thick stack of paper at the bra thief?"

"I don't remember exactly, but yes, I think there might've been some paper."

"Why didn't you stop me? That was the final draft of Yu Mogwo's manuscript with all his handwritten notes!" Chui Yuk's face grew long.

"Are you sure?"

"Was there anything written on them?" Chui Yuk grabbed my hand.

"I wasn't paying attention. Maybe they were blank."

"Right. Maybe they were blank." She let out a breath of relief.

It was two in the morning by the time I got home. Would the bra thief change his ways? I doubted it. A fetish was a kind of attachment. If he were forced to give up stealing bras, he might lose all sense of meaning in his life.

I sat down at the dining-room table and began working on the jigsaw puzzle. By four in the morning, I'd finished all four edges. I heard a knock on the door. When I went to open it, I found Chui Yuk holding a pile of paper. She was crying her eyes out.

"The paper I threw wasn't blank. It was Mogwo's final draft of his novel and all his notes. He'd promised to hand it over to the publisher tomorrow," Chui Yuk said.

"Did you two have a fight?"

"When I got home, Yu Mogwo was terrified. He said he thought there'd been some kind of accident when he came home from work only to discover the manuscript pages of his novel were scattered outside the entrance of the building. Most of his work is lost. I told him that I just grabbed whatever was around to throw at the thief, but he wouldn't listen to a word I said. He spent so much time working on that novel. It's all my fault."

"Why'd you come all the way over here? Did he throw you out?"

"He didn't throw me out. Since I didn't want to see him go, I had to be the one to leave. He's never gotten this upset with me before. I'm scared he's going to break up with me."

"He won't," I said in an attempt to console her.

"This time, it's really serious." Chui Yuk was choking back sobs.

"I know. Because it's out of your hands."

"Will we ever put this night behind us?"

"Of course you will. You can sleep here with me tonight."

"Thanks," she said. Then she moved over to my table. "You're putting together a puzzle?"

"I don't know when I'll be done with it. This is the restaurant that Sam and I want to open. But I'm worried that by the time I finish it, we'll have split up."

"Do you want to marry him?"

"That's never going to happen. Men who've been married before don't want to get hitched again. They wouldn't want to make the same mistake twice, would they?"

"How much of your youth can you afford to squander like this?" Chui Yuk asked. "I just don't want you to have any regrets."

I lent Chui Yuk a pair of pajamas.

"Since this is our first time sharing a bed," I told Chui Yuk, "I should really tell you that this is going to be the first time I've ever slept with anyone in this bed at night. It's always after the break of dawn when Sam is here."

"I bet you anything Yu Mogwo is working on his manuscript right now," Chui Yuk said, putting her pager down next to the bed.

When I woke up the following morning, Chui Yuk was already gone.

On the dining-room table was a note she'd left for me.

"I can't stop thinking about Yu Mogwo. I have to go."

The phone rang. I thought it was going to be Chui Yuk, but it was Sam.

"Where were you last night?" he asked me.

"Were you looking for me? I went to catch a bra thief."

"Did someone steal your bra?"

"No, I was helping Chui Yuk."

"Are you OK?"

"I'd be OK if you were here."

"So what happened in the end?"

"Nothing. They hauled him off to the police station. I really wished you were there with me."

"I'll join you for dinner tonight."

That day felt like an eternity. I spent my whole life waiting for Sam—waiting for him to call me and waiting to see him.

I met him at a French bistro in Central.

"Why did you want to come here?" I asked him.

"One of my colleagues recommended it. What do you think?"

"It's not as nice as our restaurant, of course," I said, laughing.

"Please promise me that you won't go around catching any more thieves for no good reason," Sam said.

"Will you always be there to protect me?"

"I'm never going to leave you," he said.

"That's too bad. Because I won't always be there for you," I said.

"What?"

"Didn't I say that a woman is only young once? I can only be with you until I'm thirty."

"Why thirty?"

"Because a woman is at the height of her attractiveness before she turns thirty. After that, I'll have to watch out for myself," I said.

2

Skies over Cherbourg

"There's something I want to give you," Sam told me just before he left that evening.

"What is it?"

He took a velvet box out of his bag. It contained a crystal pendant in the shape of a ball. Inside the ball was a scorpion.

"I thought a scorpion would suit you perfectly."

He hung it around my neck.

"Scorpions are lonely," I said.

"You're not lonely—you have me," he said, putting his arms around me.

"I can't stand to see you go." I clung to him tightly. But I knew he had to leave.

"Are you going to spend my birthday with me this year?" I asked.

He nodded lightly, and I let him go on his way, suddenly happier.

***

During class that evening, Chen Dingleung's eyes were watering non-stop, and I gathered he was suffering from a severe cold.

"Did you find that song?" I asked him.

"No, I couldn't find it," he said.

I was a little disappointed.

"That's a lovely pendant you're wearing," he said.

"Thank you."

"Is it a scorpion?"

"Yes." I turned to leave.

"All I could find were the lyrics," he said, pulling a sheet of paper out of his backpack. "The only problem is they're in French."

"I don't speak French."

"I do. I can translate them for you."

"I'd appreciate it."

"How about we go sit down somewhere? I'd love a cup of honey lemon tea."

"I'm meeting a friend at a restaurant near here. Would you like to join us?" I'd made plans with Chui Yuk after class.

"Sounds good."

At the restaurant, he ordered a cup of tea, and I waited expectantly for him to read the lyrics to me. He took out a handkerchief and wiped his eyes and nose.

"How are you feeling?" I asked.

"I've had a bad cold for the last few days." He seemed to realize I was impatient to hear the translation because he said, "Are the words to this song really important to you?"

I smiled but didn't say a word as he translated out loud to me.

"That's it?" I asked, considering the song's sentiment of not being able to live without that special someone. But before I could ask Chen Dingleung about what he thought it meant, Chui Yuk appeared behind him.

"Let me introduce you. This is Chen Dingleung, my teacher. This is Chui Yuk. She's a model. He's translating lyrics for me."

"You two sounded like you were having an intense discussion," Chui Yuk said.

"How did you find the lyrics?" I asked Chen Dingleung.

"I can't remember whether someone wrote them down for me, or if I wrote them down to give to someone else. It was a long time ago. Here, you can have them."

"This doesn't look like your handwriting," I said.

"Someone else must have written them down for me, then."

"Was it someone who was waiting for you?" I asked, giggling.

Chen Dingleung wiped his nose. "It was more than ten years ago. She's probably married now. Who'd wait forever for someone?"

"Some women can keep waiting for a man," I said.

"Women can, but men can't."

"Why can't men wait?"

"Because men are men." Chen Dingleung shook his head, laughing.

"Maybe you can't wait, but you can't speak for all men."

"Do you have a man waiting for you?"

"What does that have to do with anything?"

"When you're waiting for a man, do you sleep with other men?"

"That's not waiting," Chui Yuk said.

"Well, a man can keep waiting and sleep with other women at the same time." Chen Dingleung took out his handkerchief again and wiped his nose.

"You can't speak for all men."

"No, but I have more say in the matter than you do. It's women that I can't speak for."

"Is it really true that a man can wait for a woman and have relationships with other women at the same time?" Chui Yuk asked.

"He can—even if he's married. Men don't see any conflict between those two things."

"No conflict?" I sneered.

"Of course there's no conflict. That's why a man can love two different women at the same time."

I was momentarily speechless. Maybe Chen Dingleung was right. Maybe Sam could live with one woman and still love another. It seemed that men were truly capable of going back and forth between two women without any sort of inner conflict.

"So, according to what you're saying, no man would wait forever for a woman," Chui Yuk said.

"That's not true," Chen Dingleung said, wiping his eyes with his handkerchief.

"There are men who would wait forever for a woman," Chen Dingleung said.

"Is that so?" His sudden turnabout surprised me.

"Because they can't get another one," he said coolly.

"If all men were like you, there'd be no romantic love stories," Chui Yuk said.

"You believe in romantic love stories?" Chen Dingleung asked her.

Chui Yuk nodded.

"Well, you're a woman. That would explain it," Chen Dingleung said.

"I'm hungry. Should we order some food?" I asked.

"I'm in the mood for minced meat noodles," said Chui Yuk.

"What about you?" I asked Chen Dingleung.

"I don't want to be in the way of whatever you two had planned."

I shook my head to indicate he wasn't interfering with our plans.

"I'll have another cup of honey lemon tea," he said.

"What do you want to eat?"

"I'm not hungry."

After finishing his second cup of honey lemon tea, Chen Dingleung fell asleep in his chair. His nostrils emitted a faint snoring sound with each breath, probably because he was so congested. His mouth fell slightly open, and his body slouched towards Chui Yuk.

"Should we wake him up?" Chui Yuk asked.

"No, he seems really sick. Let him sleep for a while. Did you and Yu Mogwo make up?"

"He didn't sleep a wink after I left the apartment that night."

"What about his novel?"

"He's starting over and writing a new one." Chui Yuk took out a book and announced, "This is Yu Mogwo's new book."

"It's already done?"

"It's part of a collection," Chui Yuk said.

"Is it from the same mom-and-pop publisher? I thought you said they weren't any good." The cover was mediocre, and the print job looked rather shoddy.

"There's nothing we can do about it. Major publishing houses want big-name authors. They don't go around searching for up-and-coming talent. It's their loss. As long as the work is good, there'll be people who appreciate it." Chui Yuk was brimming with confidence.

"All right. I'll take it home and read it."

"People are going to love it. I've read it several times already."

Chui Yuk and I talked for nearly an hour while Chen Dingleung slept soundly. When it was time to go, I patted his shoulder hard, and his eyes fluttered open.

"Oh, I'm so sorry," he said and began digging through his bag for his wallet.

"I already paid," I said.

"Why, thank you. I'll take you home."

"Chui Yuk lives in Western. Can you drop her off after me?"

"Of course."

"There isn't a woman waiting for you at home, is there?" Chui Yuk asked mockingly.

"You women never let an argument go, do you?" Chen Dingleung said, shaking his head.

***

As Chen Dingleung drove, he glanced at the book in my hand.

"Yu Mogwo, eh? I've read a book of his."

"You have?" Chui Yuk asked, suddenly excited.

"It was good."

"Yu Mogwo is Chui Yuk's boyfriend," I said.

"Really? Can I borrow that book?" Chen Dingleung asked me.

"Sure, you can read it first if you like."

"How did you hear about Yu Mogwo?" Chui Yuk asked him.

Our jeep passed through a tunnel, heading straight for Chui Yuk's neighborhood.

"Aren't you supposed to drop me off in Central first?" I asked.

"Oh! I forgot."

"It's OK, there's no rush. You can drop off Chui Yuk first."

"You were asking me how I heard about Yu Mogwo," Chen Dingleung said to Chui Yuk. "I was initially drawn to the name."

I laughed.

"What's so funny?" Chen Dingleung asked.

"Do you know what the name Yu Mogwo means? It means 'It was written in the stars.'"

"Like 'If the bra fits, wear it'?" Chui Yuk started giggling.

Chui Yuk regained her composure. "Yu Mogwo's very first novel was a story about human beings invading a weaker planet. But the weaker planet had done nothing wrong. It was the human beings who were at fault. That's where his pen name comes from."

"Trust me. It's a good pen name. It's lucky," I said with a laugh.

"I know it is." Chui Yuk looked proud.

"But the book cover design wasn't very good," Chen Dingleung said.

"I know. But there was nothing we could do about it. They just didn't have money in the budget for a designer," Chui Yuk said.

"I'll design the next one for you," Chen Dingleung said.

"Really?" Chui Yuk grabbed Chen Dingleung's arm.

"His fees are high," I said.

"Don't worry, I won't charge you," Chen Dingleung said.

"You're such a wonderful person. I had you all wrong earlier," Chui Yuk said.

She thanked Chen Dingleung profusely when he dropped her off at her place before taking me home.

As soon as I walked in the door, I got a phone call from Chui Yuk.

"Does Chen Dingleung like you?"

"I don't know. Do you think so?"

"He deliberately took the wrong road and dropped you off last. Wasn't it obvious that he wanted to be alone with you? I only met him for the first time tonight, and he suddenly volunteered to design the cover of Yu Mogwo's book. He's not doing it for my sake, is he?"

"This is only the second time I've met him myself."

"It might be love at first sight—watch out!"

"He and I have the same birthday."

"Really?"

"Believe me, I was just as surprised as you."

"Are fashion designers usually the licentious type?"

"It sounds like Chen Dingleung has a lot of experience with women," I said.

"Don't reject him," Chui Yuk admonished me.

"Why?"

"Because if you reject him, then he won't design the cover of Yu Mogwo's next book. Just put up with him for a bit. Please, I'm begging you."

"That's totally preposterous. You only care about yourself."

"This is actually for your own good, too. Do you think you're still so young? Sooner or later, a woman has to think about getting married."

"How do you know Chen Dingleung doesn't have a wife? I'm not making the same mistake twice."

I took the sheet of lyrics that Chen Dingleung had given me out of my purse and slid it underneath the jigsaw puzzle. I said I'd leave Sam when I turned thirty. Now this Chen Dingleung character, with whom I shared a birthday, had appeared. Was that just a coincidence? Based on what I'd seen so far, my feminine intuition told me he wasn't awful. And I knew he didn't dislike me. A woman always wants to be liked by a man, especially one who's considered a real catch. I took off my necklace and dangled it under the light. The scorpion inside the crystal ball was me, and the crystal ball was Sam. There'd never be another man who'd protect me the way Sam did. Losing one was already enough.

Just then, the phone rang. I picked up, but whoever it was immediately hung up. I'd been getting a lot of these silent hoax calls recently.

One morning a few days later, I received a phone call.

"Hello? Who is this?"

"This is Sam's wife, Mrs. Tong."

I was stunned.

"Those silent hoax calls you've been getting? Those were from me," she said. "How long have you and Sam known each other?"

"Mrs. Tong, I don't know what you're talking about." Denying it was the only thing I could think to do at that moment.

"Don't bother denying it. Sam and I dated for ten years. We've now been married for seven. He's changed a lot in the past four years. I know he lies to me every day. How do you know him?"

"Aren't I entitled to any privacy?"

"Privacy, eh?" She let out a cold laugh. "I trust that you two haven't gone so far as to do anything improper?"

She was genuinely deluded.

"Does he love you?" she asked me.

"I can't answer for him," I said.

"He doesn't love me anymore," she said soberly.

She was so calm and matter-of-fact about it that I felt a twinge of guilt.

"Can you promise that you won't tell him about our conversation today?" she asked.

"I promise."

I hung up the phone and sat down at the dining-room table. I picked up a piece of the puzzle and put it in its place. I thought I'd cry, but I didn't. The day had finally come, and I'd been freed of all my doubts. Sam didn't love two different women at the same time; he only loved me.

Sam called at dusk. He said he'd join me for dinner.

We ate at a yakitori restaurant. Sam had just made a huge profit on a trade and was in a great mood. I had no idea what that other woman would do, and I was afraid that this might be the last time we'd ever see each other. I snuggled up close to Sam, putting my leg on his lap.

Though I didn't necessarily have to keep my word, I didn't want her to hate me and think that I was just trying to bad-mouth her.

The following morning, Sam didn't call me, and I started to worry. But that afternoon, I finally heard from him.

"Do you have something to tell me?" he asked me.

It appeared that I was the one who was naive. I had thought that she would keep our little chat a secret, too.

"Last night, she went stark raving mad," he said.

"So what do we do now?"

He was silent for a long time.

"You can't see me anymore?" I asked him.

"I'll call you soon," he said.

I hung up, terrified that he'd never call me again.

***

That evening, I went to my fashion design class.

Chen Dingleung asked us to make sketches of our designs. I drew a long black evening gown with diamond-encrusted shoulder straps. The dress was backless, and there was a giant bow in the back, at the waist. I was feeling grumpy. I went through sheet after sheet of paper before I finally got it down. Even so, it still wasn't quite how I had imagined it. I crumpled up my sheet of paper and chucked it into the trash can.

Class ended. As I exited the classroom, Chen Dingleung caught up to me.

"I finished reading Yu Mogwo's book. I can give it back to you."

I saw that he was empty-handed.

"It's in my car. Are you heading to the other side of the harbor?"

I nodded.

"You don't seem to be in a very good mood this evening," he remarked as we approached his car. He opened the door for me.

"A woman doesn't need to explain why she's in a bad mood," I told him, getting in.

We pulled up to my place in silence.

"Hold on." He hopped out of the jeep and went to the rear hatch. He came back with two gigantic watermelons. "Today I went up north, to the outskirts of town, to see my mother—she lives in Fanling. She gave me these. I can't eat them both by myself, so let me give you one."

"Thank you." I stepped out of the car and held out both hands.

"It's a pretty heavy watermelon. I'll take it up for you."

Fancy that—he was using the watermelon as a pretext to come up to my apartment.

Chen Dingleung carried up the watermelon and put it in my refrigerator.

He looked at my jigsaw puzzle. "A fifth of the way done already?"

I checked my wristwatch. It was 10:05. Sam was probably still at the office.

"My ex-wife got remarried today," Chen Dingleung said.

So Chen Dingleung was divorced. Today probably wasn't a good day for him, either. We had the same birthday, and we were in a bad mood on the same day.

"How come you didn't go to the wedding?"

"Because she didn't invite me."

"So how do you know she got remarried?"

"My mother told me. My ex-wife and my mother are on slightly better terms." Chen Dingleung let out a bitter laugh.

"So your divorce definitely wasn't the result of mother-in-law problems," I said, smiling.

"It was the result of my own problems."

"I don't understand marriage," I said.

"I don't understand marriage, either. But I understand divorce."

"Divorce is an agonizing ordeal."

Did Sam feel the same way—that breaking up was even harder than making a commitment?

"It's getting late," Chen Dingleung said. "I'd better be going."

"Thanks for the watermelon."

"I almost forgot—Yu Mogwo's book." Chen Dingleung pulled Yu Mogwo's book out of his pocket and handed it to me.

"Was it good?"

"It was pretty good, though I wouldn't say it's first-rate."

"How many first-rate books are there in the world, anyway?" I muttered as he waved good-bye. As far as I was concerned, the two of us had nothing to talk about.

When Chen Dingleung left, I felt incredibly lonely. I had never imagined that he'd be so kind and open with me. I stared at the clock, watching the minutes and seconds pass, and then it was three in the morning. I wondered if Sam was at home, promising his wife that he'd never see me again.

I got up and hurried to get dressed. Then I headed over to Sam's office, where I paced back and forth outside. I'd never done anything like it before. I didn't even know if he was in there.

I was the only person on the street at that dark and desolate hour. Why couldn't I just give up? Why couldn't I accept the fact that this love was destined to perish sooner or later? It was agonizing.

I don't know how long I'd been waiting when several men emerged from the bank. I didn't see Sam among them. Maybe he wasn't even at work.

Ten minutes later, Sam suddenly came out of the bank.

"What are you doing here?" he asked when he saw me.

"I missed you!" I cried, running into his arms.

"Shouldn't you be asleep at this hour?"

"I couldn't sleep. Are you planning to never see me again?'

"Let me take you home."

It was four in the morning, and except for the rare early bird, there wasn't a soul to be seen in Central. We held hands. Out of nowhere, I was struck by a feeling: Sam wasn't going to leave me.

"I didn't startle you, did I?" I asked Sam.

"I'm lucky I didn't have a heart attack."

"I'm sorry. I should've told you that she called," I said.

"Well, she knows everything now."

"Did you promise her that you'd never see me again?"

"When I want something, no one's going to stop me."

"So that means that either you don't want to get divorced, or that you can't get divorced, right?"

"Where's a thirty-seven-year-old woman supposed to go after she gets divorced?"

"Oh, so that's how it is. I'd rather be thirty-seven than be me," I said. I understood what he meant, though—a woman could use her age to gain protection in a marriage.

"What are we going to do now?" I asked Sam.

"Just don't use your own name anymore when you call me. Use the name Chui instead."

"Why Chui?" I asked, feeling hurt.

"It was just a thought. Since it's your best friend's name, you know."

"Fine. So am I Mr. or Ms. Chui?" I snickered.

"It's up to you. Just don't leave your phone number—I don't want her to be able to track you down."

"Why are you so afraid of her?"

"I just don't want anyone to get hurt."

Sam rested both of his hands on my shoulders and said, "I'm never going to leave you."

I weakened a bit at those words.

"Great! I'll just change my phone number so she can't ever reach me again."

When we got back to my building, Sam and I parted ways, and I lay awake in bed. Any remotely intelligent woman would understand that now was the time to leave. Otherwise, she'd have wasted her youth and be forevermore resigned to being a secret paramour. But I was clearly willing to change my name to Chui at the drop of a hat. Sometimes I really hated myself.

Sam's birthday was fast approaching. I spent every day working on the puzzle. On Sunday, Chui Yuk came over and complained that I was completely preoccupied with it.

"There are people you can hire to do puzzles for you," Chui Yuk said.

"I want every single piece to be assembled with my own hands."

"How will he ever know?"

"Let's not get into that."

"Yu Mogwo has been acting strange recently," Chui Yuk said. "He seems to be under a lot of pressure. He's been writing nonstop. He's even started smoking."

"That explains why you smell like cigarette smoke."

"I'm worried about him."

"I've never heard of anyone going insane from writing."

That night I took a bath, then sat down at the dining-room table. I could already see the skies over Cherbourg, along with Cherbourg's roads and most of the restaurant. There was only about a quarter of the restaurant left, along with the proprietor and proprietress.

I worked on the puzzle relentlessly until the owners were done. Only when I smelled the scent of cake from downstairs did I realize that I'd worked all the way through the night. I laid the final piece of the puzzle in its place. It was the proprietor's chest.

Finally, I was finished. I couldn't recall how many hours I'd spent on it, but in the end, I had before me what we'd described as our restaurant. When the time came, Sam would do the cooking, and I'd serve the customers. After lunchtime, we'd sit around, leisurely chatting away.

Before I headed to work, I went to Ms. Kwok's cake shop to place an order.

"This is the first time you've ordered a cake!" she said.

"It's for my friend's birthday."

"What kind of cake are you interested in?"

"Is it true that you can make any kind of design?"

"It depends on how difficult it is."

I handed her the box for the jigsaw puzzle. "Can you put this restaurant on top of the cake?"

"This restaurant?" She seemed startled.

"Oh, never mind. It's probably too complicated."

"When do you need it?"

"Tomorrow."

After work, Sam called me.

"Are we going to spend tomorrow together?" I asked him.

"What's tomorrow?"

"Tomorrow's your birthday. Did you forget?"

"I actually did forget. The only thing I can remember is today's market value for the British pound."

"So does that mean you're not spending tomorrow with me? If you can't, it's no big deal."

"What time tomorrow?"

"It's up to you."

"I'll pick you up at seven."

After Sam hung up, Chui Yuk called.

"There's definitely something wrong with Yu Mogwo. He hasn't been able to write a thing these past few days." Chui Yuk sounded deeply distressed.

"Sort of like how most people get constipated."

"We've hardly crossed paths over the last few weeks."

"Too much of a good thing sometimes makes you sick of it. Don't let your imagination get carried away."

As I tried to comfort Chui Yuk, I also gave some thought to what I should wear tomorrow. The occasion called for a new pair of panties, and I used my employee discount to buy a corset as well. It went perfectly with the black skirt I'd just bought.

That morning, I went to the cake shop to pick up my order. The cake looked absolutely incredible. The design really did bear a remarkable likeness to the restaurant in Cherbourg.

"I tried my best," Ms. Kwok said.

"It's beautiful. Thank you so much."

I put the cake in my refrigerator and hid the finished jigsaw puzzle, which I'd framed. Then I went to work. I left work two hours earlier than usual so that I could have my hair done at a salon, and, on a whim, I bought a bottle of red wine on my way home. It was already 7:15 p.m.

by the time I reached my building. I got there just in time to see Sam coming out.

"I've been waiting for you for a long time," he said.

"I . . . I was having my hair done."

"I'm sorry," he said.

"What do you mean by that?" My body started shaking uncontrollably.

Sam looked at me, not saying a word.

"You said seven. It's only a quarter past. I went to pick up a bottle of wine. It's for you." I took the bottle out of the bag and showed it to him.

"I can't spend the evening with you."

I stared at him indignantly.

"She organized a dinner tonight with several of our friends and family," Sam said.

"You promised me." I glared at him, then dashed inside.

He didn't follow me upstairs. He wasn't coming after me; he really had gone home.

I drank the entire bottle of red wine. I pulled the jigsaw puzzle out of the closet, took it out of its frame, and slid it onto the floor. With both hands, I overturned it, letting the pieces scatter in all directions. It filled me with glee to destroy something I'd made with my own hands. He'd shattered our agreement, so I'd shattered his present. It was easier to destroy something than to make it in the first place.

Right. And then there was the cake in the refrigerator. I took it out. The box hadn't been opened, and a ribbon was tied around it.

I took the cake over to Chui Yuk's apartment and knocked.

"Happy birthday," I said when she opened the door.

Chui Yuk froze for about three seconds. I thrust the cake into her hands.

"What happened?" she asked me.

"I need to use the bathroom!"

I stormed inside. For a long time, I was propped up against the toilet, throwing up. I heard Chui Yuk calling for Yu Mogwo to come help. The two of them brought me over to the sofa, and Chui Yuk made me a cup of tea.

"Aren't you supposed to be having dinner with Sam?" Chui Yuk asked. My head felt much clearer after vomiting. It was only then that I noticed that Yu Mogwo's appearance had changed. His hair was a mess, he was sporting a full beard, and he looked like he'd lost a lot of weight. A cigarette dangled out of the corner of his mouth.

"What's happened to you?" I couldn't help asking.

"You two can talk. I have to work on my book," Yu Mogwo said coldly.

"What's happened to him?" I asked Chui Yuk.

"I already told you. This all started about a month ago. He's been locking himself up in the study to work on his new manuscript. Plus he quit his job today and said he's going to stay home and write."

"What prompted all of this?"

"I think the newspaper stopped publishing his fiction right around that time. He was pretty unhappy about it. He's put all this pressure on himself to write a bestseller. As a result, he's so stressed out that he can't even write anymore. His moods have been getting worse and worse."

"Everyone has their own troubles." I suddenly had a terrible headache.

"Why did you drink so much?"

"That woman did it on purpose. She organized a dinner tonight with all their friends and family to celebrate Sam's birthday so that he couldn't spend the evening with me."

"What are you going to do now?"

"It never used to get to me, but I'm not like that anymore. I can't lose out to her. It's up to me to fight it out with her until the very end."

"You? Why is it up to you?"

"I know I'm the one Sam really loves," I said.

"So why isn't he with you today, then?"

I didn't have an answer. It was true. Even if he did love me, what good was that? He'd always be at her side, no matter what.

"Chow Jeoi, you're the other woman!"

Chui Yuk's words were a major wake-up call. I absolutely loathed the thought of myself as the other woman. All this time, I'd been trying to convince myself that his wife was actually the other woman. She was the one who was making it impossible for Sam and me to get married. Now that I was being confronted with the cold, hard facts, though, it was pretty laughable.

"I feel bad. That was never my intention."

Chui Yuk sat down next to me, wrapping her hands around her knees. "For love, I'd be willing to be the other woman, too. So it's settled, then. You and I are both people who act on their emotions. People like that suffer."

"Can I stay over tonight? I don't want to go home."

"Of course you can. You can sleep next to me."

"What about Yu Mogwo?"

"He's been sleeping in the study for the past two weeks," Chui Yuk said glumly.

I lay down in Chui Yuk's bed and drifted into a muddled sleep. In the middle of the night, my bladder felt like it was ready to explode, so I got up to go to the bathroom. The door to the study was halfway open, and I could see Yu Mogwo, his back turned towards me. He was sitting at a desk, crumpling sheet after sheet of manuscript paper and tossing it on the floor. The floor was practically covered in crumpled balls of paper. He turned around and stared at me. His expression was blank. He was about to become the first person to go insane while writing a novel.

***

In the morning, I woke up Chui Yuk.

"I'm leaving now."

"Where are you going?"

"If I don't go to work, I can't pay the bills."

"Do you feel any better?"

"I decided I'm going to break up with Sam," I said.

"Break up with him? This isn't the first time you've said that." Chui Yuk didn't seem to believe me.

"This time it's for real. I thought it all through last night. You were right. I'm the other woman. That's never going to change—ever," I said miserably.

"Can you really bring yourself to leave him?"

"I don't want to hear his lies anymore. I don't want to be disappointed anymore. Being deceived by the person you love is a painful ordeal."

"I don't know. I'm often deceived by people I like," Chui Yuk said with a wry laugh.

"I'm going to move back in with my family for a while."

"Why?"

"I don't want to see Sam. I don't want to give myself a chance to change my mind."

Just then, my pager went off. It was Sam. As I left Chui Yuk's apartment, I shut off my pager.

Though we'd broken up numerous times before over the past four years, none of those times had been for real. This time it was different. I felt something like hopelessness. I'd cried all the other times, but this time I didn't. I went home and packed up my clothes. The pieces of the jigsaw puzzle lay scattered on the floor. Our restaurant would never materialize. The phone rang. I sat beside it, waiting for it to stop ringing. I knew it was Sam. The phone wouldn't stop ringing. He must've thought I was still mad. I left, pulling my suitcase behind me. As I went past the first floor, I ran into Ms. Kwok.

"Going on a vacation, Ms. Chow?" she asked me, smiling.

"Yes."

"How was the cake?"

I nodded a little. I hadn't even tried it.

When I got to the store, Anna said that Sam had called for me. His fretting over me only made me more resolved to leave him. The phone rang again, and I picked up the receiver.

"Where were you?" he asked me.

"Happy birthday," I said.

"How about if I come over tonight?"

"Forget it. I'm done listening to your lies."

"Let's talk about it tonight."

"No. I don't want to see you. I'm moving out of that apartment. I'm grateful for the time we had together. Good-bye." I hung up.

Sam didn't call me back. I didn't think I'd ever have the courage to break up with him. I'd never loved anyone that much before. But now it was time to let him go.

That night in class, Chen Dingleung noticed my suitcase.

"Are you catching a red-eye?"

"No."

"I'll take you across the harbor."

"Thanks, but I'm not going across the harbor."

"I have something to give you," Chen Dingleung said, handing me a cassette. "It's the song you wanted, 'I Will Wait for You.'"

I hadn't expected to get that song at that particular moment. My face went blank. Why was I always so slow on the uptake?

"What, did you find it already?" he asked.

"Oh, no. Thank you. How'd you find it?"

"I have my ways."

***

Later that night, back at my mother's house, I dropped the tape into the cassette player and pressed "Play."

"I will wait for you . . ." Sorry Sam, I thought, I can't wait for you.

For the next two weeks, I stayed at my mother's house. Sam didn't come looking for me there, and he didn't stop by the lingerie shop. I'd been hoping that he'd call or maybe come to the store. But he didn't. Even though I was the one to break up with him, I actually felt a little disappointed. How could he have given up so soon? Maybe he knew that there was no point. It wasn't that I wouldn't change my mind; it was that there was no way for him to change reality.

Chui Yuk and I went to the movies, where we watched a sidesplitting comedy together. While Chui Yuk cracked up loudly, I didn't even smile.

"You were the one who wanted to end it, so he didn't come looking for you. And yet you're unhappy about it," Chui Yuk said.

"Even if you tell a man that you want to break up with him, aren't you allowed to want him to beg you to stay?"

"You're still wearing the necklace he gave you."

It was true. I couldn't bring myself to take off the necklace.

"You don't think something happened to him, do you? It seems so unlike him not to try to reach me at all," I said.

"No, I don't think there's been a freak accident. If you're so worried, you can always reach out to him."

"He's so sneaky. He's probably backing off like this just to draw me in. He knows I won't be able to resist being the one to get in touch first."

"Whatever you say."

"I want to go home and see."

"Do you want me to go with you? Just in case Sam committed suicide there . . ."

"He'd never die for me."

***

I went back to my apartment to see whether Sam had stopped by and maybe left something for me. But everything was just as I'd left it. The only difference was that the puzzle pieces that I'd left on the floor were missing. The puzzle was sitting on the dining-room table, fully completed.

How could it be? I distinctly remembered tossing it on the floor and letting it crumble to pieces. Who could have put it back together?

Sam stepped out of the bathroom.

"When did you get here?" I asked him.

"Two weeks ago."

"Two weeks ago?" I asked him.

He walked up to the puzzle and said, "I just finished putting it back together."

"Have you been coming here every day?"

"Every day. Whenever I had a little free time, I came and worked on the puzzle," Sam said.

"How did you get it done so quickly?"

"I told you I had a knack for puzzles. This one was pretty challenging, though. If I hadn't had two whole weeks to work on it, I never would've gotten it done."

"Why'd you do it?" I asked him, tears welling in my eyes.

"It's our restaurant." Sam put his arms around me.

"Get away from me!" The tears started to trickle down my cheeks as I tried to push him away.

"The night you told me you wanted to break up, I came over here. When I saw the puzzle scattered in pieces on the floor, I wanted to put it back together. I thought that if you came back someday, you'd see the puzzle and it would make you happy."

"You thought I'd come back?"

"No. I thought you wouldn't come back. I was sure that you'd always think I'd deceived you. There have been times when I felt I was being selfish and that I should set you free, so that you could find a man who'd take care of you for the rest of your life."

"But you couldn't bring yourself to let me go? I can't stand you! I truly cannot stand you. In fact, I've never hated someone as much as I hate you right now." I charged at him, yanking his shirtsleeves and swinging my fists at him.

Sam pulled me close and held me tight.

"I can't stand you!" I said, crying.

"I know," he said.

I hugged Sam with all my might. I truly couldn't stand him, especially since I now knew that there was no way on earth I could ever truly leave him. I clung to him, this man whom I hadn't seen in fourteen long days, this man who provided strength and warmth and yet could make me feel so much pain. Love is such a devastating force sometimes that what we call reason and willpower amount to no more than meager words of consolation.

3
Flying Backwards

"Yu Mogwo is leaving!"

Chui Yuk arrived just as I was closing up the shop.

"Where's he going?"

"He's going to study in the States."

"Going to study?"

"He heard about a creative-writing program. Michael Crichton took classes there, and he went on to write *Congo* and *Jurassic Park*."

"Oh, really?"

"Yu Mogwo had me really scared there for a while, but he's been much better over the last few days. He said his inspiration has run dry, so he needs a change of scene."

"That's good news. Otherwise he might be the first person to ever spiral into madness while writing a science-fiction novel."

"The thing is, he insists on going by himself."

"By himself? For how long?"

"All he said was he's going for as long as he's going."

"Does he want to break up with you?"

Chui Yuk looked at me helplessly. She couldn't hold back the single tear that trickled down her cheek. "He didn't say he wanted to break up. He said he wanted to try out a different way of life because his current life is slowly killing him. Maybe I'm standing in the way of his artistic pursuits. Is it possible that a writer can have too much emotional stability?"

I didn't know how to answer that. I thought that a writer was just like anyone else who was always shifting between stability and instability, and occasionally finding a balance. One thing was certain, though. The nature of Yu Mogwo and Chui Yuk's love was changing. He was starting to pull away from her; he was looking for a way out. There were only two possible outcomes: he would eventually realize that Chui Yuk was the woman he loved most, or he would eventually break up with her.

When Chui Yuk opened her purse and took out a tissue to wipe away her tears, I noticed that she had an awful lot of cash inside of her purse.

"Why are you carrying around so much money?"

"I went to the bank and withdrew it for Yu Mogwo."

"Is that your savings?"

Chui Yuk nodded. "I have tens of thousands of dollars in here. It's my entire savings."

"He has some nerve using up all your savings to go on a vacation like that," I said.

"He's not going on vacation. He's going to clear his mind. Yu Mogwo has always been the strong-willed type. You haven't lived with him, so you just haven't seen it, that's all. He always has to have his way. It doesn't matter how other people feel. I'm his girlfriend, which means I'm always trailing behind him, picking up the pieces. When the publisher calls to find out whether his manuscript is ready, I'm the one who has to answer to them. If he curses someone out, I'm the one who has to apologize. If he doesn't want to get up and go to work, I'm the one who has to call in sick for him. I still haven't even introduced him to my family because I know how much he hates to socialize with other people."

I shook my head, laughing darkly.

"What's so funny?"

"Yu Mogwo and I are more similar than I realized. I used to be the more strong-willed one. And it used to be Sam who picked up the pieces for me. Now that I think about it, I was lucky."

"I don't think of myself as being unlucky! I like taking care of Yu Mogwo. I feel like he needs me, and that's really important."

I was different from Chui Yuk. I wasn't used to taking care of someone else. I liked being taken care of. To me, it was really important to feel like I was being taken care of.

"When's Yu Mogwo leaving?"

"Soon."

"So what are you going to do?"

"He promised he'd call me once he was settled. My mind's been spinning ever since I found out, but if you love someone, you have to give them space, right?"

"You're so very wise."

If there was ever a woman who relied on love and loss to mature and grow as a person, Chui Yuk was that woman.

Two weeks later, Yu Mogwo left in search of freedom and inspiration—with Chui Yuk's entire savings in hand. Chui Yuk fought back tears as she took him to the airport. Yu Mogwo left without so much as a second thought. I still believed that being taken care of was much better than taking care of someone else. As long as someone's trailing behind you, picking up the pieces, why not do whatever the hell you feel like?

Today was the start of our semiannual sale, and the store was full of customers who weren't usually willing to spend money on expensive lingerie but would come in if there was a sale.

At dusk, a really skinny woman came into the store. Her face looked familiar, but I couldn't quite place where I'd seen her before. She wasn't the least bit curvaceous, and she looked pretty flat. I guessed she was a 32A, max. She lingered for a long time, and finally I went over to her.

"Excuse me, miss, is there anything I can help you with?"

"Do you carry . . . push-up bras?" she asked.

"Ah, yes." I'd already predicted that she was going to ask for a bra with an especially dramatic effect—which is why she waited until there weren't many other customers in the store before speaking up.

"There are three kinds of push-up bras—which kind are you looking for?" I asked her.

"There are three kinds?"

"There's maximum support, medium, and light."

"I want maximum," she said without the slightest hesitation.

"The maximum is one of our bestsellers. It can boost you up by about two cup sizes."

"Isn't that kind of like deceiving people?" She seemed a little conflicted.

"Deceiving people? Why would you say that? It's no different than wearing makeup. It's part of your beauty routine, that's all. If you put on makeup, you don't have to go around telling everybody that, do you?"

Appearing satisfied with my explanation, she asked to try one on.

"What size do you need?"

"32A," she said softly. A look of shame crossed her face.

The woman then spent about twenty minutes in the fitting room.

"Miss, do you need any help?" I asked.

"Do you think it's too much?" she asked, opening the door to her fitting room.

On the left side of her chest were five tiny birthmarks that were lined up almost in the shape of a comma. At first, I couldn't remember where I'd seen that before, but then it dawned on me.

"You're not Yau Ying, are you?"

"Chow Jeoi, is that you?"

It was all thanks to that comma.

"I recognized that comma on you," I said, pointing at her birthmarks.

"That's amazing! I was just wondering why I felt like I knew you." Yau Ying squeezed my hand. We'd known each other since we were babies. She was three months older than me, and we had been next-door neighbors. We'd gone to the same elementary school, which we walked to together every day. We'd always taken baths together as girls, which is how I recognized the comma on her chest. Back then, Yau Ying used to say it looked like an ear, but I always liked to think that it was more like a comma. To have an ear on the front of your chest would just be too weird. Yau Ying used to be really chubby, and I had imagined that she'd be a hippo by the time she grew up. It had never occurred to me that she'd turn out so skinny, which is why I didn't recognize her at first.

"You've become so thin," I told her.

"I was fat until I was ten. But when I hit puberty, I didn't have much of an appetite. That's how I ended up looking like this."

"I never thought I'd see you again. Why did you move away?"

In fifth grade, Yau Ying's family moved away very suddenly. Yau Ying stopped going to our school, and we lost touch. I still had no idea why she had gone away. I was completely crushed at the time, as I was only a kid and my best friend had disappeared out of the blue. That event cast a dark shadow across my childhood. Ever since, I'd been scared that anyone I was close to might disappear in the middle of the night without a word of explanation.

Yau Ying sat down and said, "I'll tell you what happened. My father bought a winning ticket at the horse races."

I was stunned. "A winning ticket?"

"The prize money was $1 million—and we're talking about what $1 million was worth eighteen years ago, which meant you could buy yourself a whole bunch of houses."

"So you hit the jackpot!"

"Well, yes, but my dad is an extremely paranoid person. After he won the money, he got really worried that all our relatives, friends, and neighbors would start hounding him for money—try to extort from him, kidnap his daughter, and whatnot. He got more and more paranoid, to the point where he moved all of us from Hong Kong to the New Territories in the middle of the night. My siblings and I transferred to schools there. And then he changed his name."

"So were you transformed into a little rich girl?"

"Well, not quite . . . ," she said. "My father took his million and bought only one house. At that time, no one would ever have predicted that real-estate prices would skyrocket the way they have. He used to work at a garment factory, and he wanted more than anything to have a factory of his own. So he bought one in Tsuen Wan and started his own business. For the first few years, it was very profitable. But a few years into it, he made a bad call. He thought stretch fabrics would be all the rage, and he made a huge investment in elastic bands."

"Elastic bands?" I was baffled.

Yau Ying motioned with her hands. "Elastic bands come in these huge, rough strips. Each one is about the size of a dishtowel. You can blend them with other textiles to create stretch fabrics. He was speculating on the prices of elastic bands, thinking he could make a fortune off them. He took out a mortgage on the factory and used all the money to buy elastic."

"So then what happened?"

"Stretch fabrics never came into fashion. He had to sell off the factory. All the elastic was shipped back to our house, which was packed with the stuff—the bedrooms, the dining room, the bathroom, and the kitchen were all full of elastic."

"So your father went bankrupt?"

"No. We still had our house, but my father was deeply, deeply unhappy. He eventually mortgaged the house and started another garment factory. We moved from the top of the hill in Tsuen Wan to the bottom. The money from that winning ticket lasted us only ten years."

"It sounds like your father had some bad luck. I've always wanted to go back to our old neighborhood to track you down. But it all happened so suddenly, and even if I did go, I wouldn't even have known where to begin. I never thought we'd see each other again," I said.

"Me neither! What a funny place to run into each other again."

"You must have a boyfriend!"

Yau Ying said sadly, "I do for now, but I never know if we'll still be together tomorrow."

"Why is that?"

"Love never seems to last," Yau Ying told me helplessly.

The store didn't seem like the right place to discuss this, so I suggested that we have dinner together that night.

"Sounds good! He's not coming over tonight, anyway," Yau Ying said.

That night, over Indian food at a nearby restaurant, Yau Ying handed me a photo of her snuggling up to a man.

"His name is Cheung Daihoi," she told me happily.

"He's so handsome!" I said, admiring the man's finely chiseled features.

"We've been together for seven years. He's a lawyer."

"How did you two meet?"

"We work at the same law firm. I'm the boss's secretary."

"Your name means you're a good swimmer, and his name means he's a vast ocean. You guys must be meant for each other."

"That little coincidence was part of the reason we got together."

"I just met a man who has the same birthday as I do, but there's nothing romantic between us," I said.

"Call them coincidences if you want, but they do make a relationship between two people develop a whole lot faster," Yau Ying said.

"So where does the problem lie? There isn't somebody else in the picture, is there?"

"I'm pretty confident that he doesn't have someone else. And neither do I."

"What is it, then?"

"My bust is too small . . . ," Yau Ying said.

"Your bust isn't small. For a Chinese woman, it's pretty much average. I've certainly seen smaller," I said in an effort to console Yau Ying.

Still frowning, she said, "You're bigger than me."

"I'm not so big, either. Size isn't the point, anyway. Some women have big breasts, but they sag. Some women have smaller breasts, but they're nicely shaped."

"To be honest, it makes me feel bad about myself. Daihoi said point blank that my bust is too small."

"He said that?"

"He didn't mean it in a hurtful or critical way. It just sort of accidentally slipped out, though it's happened more than once."

"But you two have been together for seven years. He didn't realize just now what your body is like, did he?"

"Of course not. The first time we hooked up, I asked him if he minded, and he said he didn't like big-breasted women. But I know that he actually does."

"As men grow older, their gaze starts to move lower—from the face to the breasts," I said, laughing. At least that was what Sam had told me.

"Chow Jeoi, there really is such a thing as a seven-year itch," Yau Ying told me earnestly. "I never used to believe it. But Daihoi and I have been together for seven years, and he's been falling asleep during sex recently. He's never, ever done that before. I discovered that he reads *Playboy*. All the photos in that magazine are of big-breasted women. The law firm recently hired a young female lawyer whose breasts are huge. Whenever she sits down to eat, her breasts rest on top of the table." Yau Ying tried to demonstrate for me. Unfortunately, her breasts didn't reach the table.

"You mean like this?" I tried to show her.

"Yes, exactly like that. Daihoi is her mentor."

I now understood why Yau Ying had bought a push-up bra.

I was no sex therapist. I didn't know how to help Yau Ying solve the sex problem between her and Daihoi. But I thought about how sex with the same partner for seven years could probably get boring, especially for a man.

"Is this really going to work?" Yau Ying asked, pointing to the bra she'd just bought.

"You tried it on today and saw for yourself!"

"Did you know that I've never bought such an expensive bra before?"

"After the sale is over, I can buy things for you using my employee discount."

"Thanks."

"I hope it works out for you!"

Yau Ying and I exchanged phone numbers. I'd never imagined that I'd see her again, or that, upon meeting, we'd have a big discussion about sexual troubles. But life was proving to be full of unexpected twists and turns.

The next day, I got a phone call from Yau Ying.

"It really works!" She sounded lovestruck.

"He told me that I looked sexy. It was the first time he'd ever used that word to describe me. He didn't fall asleep during sex last night, that's for sure!"

"So glad it did the trick! It makes you look very well-endowed!"

It hadn't occurred to me before that women's lingerie and sex therapists served the same function. A woman's once-waning sex life was now on track to regaining its vitality.

That evening in bed, I asked Sam, "Do you ever get bored?"

"Get bored of what?"

"Of my body." I sat on top of him as I spoke.

"Why do you ask?"

"If you're with the same woman's body day after day, you must get bored of it eventually."

"Says who?"

"I'm asking you."

"When I'm with you, it doesn't matter what we're doing." He pulled me close.

"You used to hold another woman in your arms. How do I know you two don't have some sort of secret agreement? Did you promise her that you'd never see me again?"

"You have a crazy imagination." He shook his head, laughing.

"So does that mean that things are going to stay the same between us?"

"How much would it cost to buy this apartment?" Sam asked.

"About $2 million."

"I'll buy it for you." He sounded sincere.

"You don't have to do that," I said.

"Why not? Don't you like it?"

"Why do you have to buy it for me?"

"Because you're the woman I love most." He kissed me.

"But I'm not your wife. Maybe you should buy it for her." I wasn't willing to let the issue drop.

"I'm indebted to you."

"You're not indebted to me. Even if you were, money is no way to make up for what you can't give me."

"I know. But I want to give you a sense of security, in case a day comes when I'm not around anymore. I want to give you a better life."

I choked back tears as I leaned over Sam. What good would it do me if I had this apartment, but I didn't have him?

"Don't cry," he said as he wiped away my tears. "Go talk to the building owner tomorrow and find out exactly how much this place would cost."

"Are you trying to give me this apartment as a breakup gift?"

Sam smiled. "There isn't a man on this planet who'd be so extravagant as to give an apartment as a parting gift. You really don't understand men."

"If someday you no longer love me, then you'll take back this apartment, right?"

"I'm not going to stop loving you. And I'm not going to take back this apartment. Why are you so suspicious of me? So now even you don't trust me?"

"No, I trust you." I put my arms around him. He probably didn't understand that bestowing such a generous gift on me would naturally send my imagination running wild.

The next day, I talked it over with Chui Yuk, who took it to mean the exact opposite. "If he's willing to buy an apartment for you, it means that he plans to be with you forever."

The building owner said he wanted $2.6 million for it. The bank would only offer a 6 percent interest rate on the mortgage.

"Don't take out a mortgage. I'll buy it with cash," Sam said.

"You're not afraid that I won't need you anymore once I get the apartment?"

"I've never doubted you."

"So will both of our names be on the deed?"

"No. My name won't be."

"Why not?" I asked him.

"It should have your name on it and that's it. If anything should happen to me, you'd lose half your property rights if my name was on it."

"If anything happened to you, this apartment would have no value to me."

"Don't be silly. You have to protect yourself. If my wife and I were to get divorced or if anything unexpectedly happened to me, she'd take half or even all of everything I own."

It was the first time that Sam had ever mentioned divorce.

"Are you going to get a divorce?"

"I'd lose everything if I did." Sam frowned.

"If money solves the problem, why not just offer her money?"

"There's more to life than money. There's the issue of doing the right thing. Would she even be able to find another man?"

Men always think they're doing the right thing. They think they're being noble by not getting divorced. They think their wives will never find other men as good as themselves. But they don't understand that if they no longer love a woman and let it drag out, it actually deprives her of an opportunity to find a better man.

"Do you think I could find a good man?" I asked him.

"Yes. You're beautiful, and lots of men would do anything to be with you." Sam took my face into his hands.

I'd always thought I was the one who was insecure. But as it turned out, Sam was even more insecure than I was. He ran things at the office with the utmost confidence, yet he was scared that a woman might up and leave him.

After our talk, he left. As I watched him head for the door, I recalled how tightly he had embraced me for fear of losing me.

"Sam!"

He turned around and looked at me. "What is it?"

Fighting back tears, I said, "I'm not going to leave you."

"You're not going to leave me when you turn thirty?" he asked, smiling.

I shook my head.

Later that day, Chui Yuk came over to the shop and gave me a set of matching bedsheets and pillowcases as a gift.

"That apartment is going to be yours from now on, so you should fix it up a little," she said.

"Has Yu Mogwo called you yet?"

"He did! He also sent me a letter," she said excitedly.

"So are things going well?"

"He says he really misses me." Chui Yuk took a letter with a US postmark on it out of her purse.

"Carrying it around with you! That must be quite a letter. Can I have a look?"

"You want to see it?" Chui Yuk looked surprised.

"I've never seen a love letter before. Plus it's a love letter from a writer! It has to be heartfelt and exhilarating, right?"

"That's right. Seeing as you're practically groveling, I'll let you take a peek."

The letter read as follows:

Yuk,

From where I am sitting, you can see many species of birds, including white doves. They all fly forwards, which prompted me to wonder: Can any birds fly backwards? I read in a book about a tiny species of bird called a hummingbird. Like a honeybee, it lives off the pollen of flowers. When it hovers near a flower, it can maintain a fixed position in the air, just like a helicopter. And it can fly backwards, though only for very short distances . . .

Being apart from you, I've been thinking back to the days when we first met. If human beings could fly backwards—just like hummingbirds—and travel back to the past, things would be perfect. As time goes on, life only grows more complicated. Now that you're not by my side, I can hardly remember all the sweet nothings that you and I used to exchange, and I often think to myself how I wish I could see you just a little sooner.

Yu Mogwo

I was jealous of Chui Yuk and her unexpectedly touching letter.

"Well?" Chui Yuk asked.

"He's a born writer, that's for sure. It's very sweet."

"I know, right? I've been reading it over and over. It makes me cry every time."

"Why don't you go see him?"

"I can't afford a plane ticket!"

"Do you need money?"

"Nope. Yu Mogwo said he wants to be left alone, and I don't want to disturb him. If I'm not by his side, he'll miss me even more. Then I hope he'll come back of his own accord."

"Right. Not being able to have a certain thing makes you want it even more badly."

"So now I understand why you and Sam get along so well."

"Sam could never write a letter like that, one that could touch the depths of someone's soul."

"But he'd buy you an apartment!"

If only Sam were a hummingbird and he could fly backwards—all the way back to before he got married—then things would be perfect! Everything really did grow more complicated as time went on. The longer he and I were together, the longer he and that other woman were also together—and the deeper their ties grew, the less likely they were to get divorced.

"What's the matter?" Chui Yuk asked me.

"I was just thinking about how hummingbirds can fly backwards."

"How do hummingbirds fly backwards, anyway? I'll ask Yu Mogwo," Chui Yuk said.

"Hummingbirds go berserk—that's how they fly backwards. All birds fly forwards!" I said, laughing.

"Who's going berserk?" Yau Ying said as she entered.

Ever since she'd started wearing her push-up bra, Yau Ying was a changed woman. There was a little extra sassiness in the way she now carried herself.

"You arrived just in time. Let me introduce you two. This is Chui Yuk. She's a good friend of mine. This is Yau Ying. We were best friends as kids, and we recently met up again."

"I know you!" Yau Ying said to Chui Yuk. "I've seen you before in bra ads!"

"She's a model," I said.

"You have such an amazing figure," Yau Ying said admiringly.

Chui Yuk couldn't help grinning. "Not really. I'm only a 36B. My figure isn't as nice as Chow Jeoi's," said Chui Yuk. "She's a nice, average 34B!"

"I really envy you both. I'm only a 32A," said Yau Ying.

"Why are you free today?" I asked Yau Ying, changing the subject.

"Daihoi has to work late tonight. I wanted to see if you were up for dinner."

"How about if we all go?"

"Sounds good," Chui Yuk said.

Once we were settled in at a nearby restaurant specializing in Shanghai cuisine, Yau Ying turned to us.

"I have a story to tell you guys about a certain 36C," she said.

"Tell us. Who is she?" I asked.

"She just so happens to be a female intern at the law firm. Her name is Olivia Wu. Ever since she came along, the male employees haven't been able to take their eyes off her."

"Does she always wear plunging necklines?" Chui Yuk asked.

"Her breasts could rest on the table," Yau Ying said with an icy laugh.

"Sounds like you really hate her—I'm guessing it's because she flirts with Daihoi, am I right?" I asked.

"Recently, she became a laughingstock," Yau Ying said. "She was wearing a loose-fitting dress, and everyone could tell that her strapless bra had slipped down underneath. She managed to yank it back up, but she'd already made a complete fool of herself!" Judging by the look on her face, Yau Ying seemed to be taking a sadistic pleasure in her colleague's moment of distress.

"Maybe she was wearing a cheap bra," I said.

Yau Ying talked about Olivia Wu all evening, and I sensed something strange about her hatred for Olivia. She kept making fun of Olivia's figure—laughing to the point of tears—and yet no tears fell. I began to think it was more a matter of jealousy than hatred.

When Chui Yuk went to the restroom, Yau Ying said, "I want to get breast implants."

"What?"

"Do you know a good plastic surgeon?"

"I've never had plastic surgery," I said, embarrassed for her.

"As you know, Daihoi likes big breasts," Yau Ying said dejectedly.

"But you have that push-up bra now."

"That's exactly what gave me the idea. I'd never have to wear a push-up bra again. I want to make him happy."

"Well, it's your body, but breast implants can come with lots of side effects. Hasn't it been proven that there are problems with silicone implants?"

"But modern medicine has made all kinds of advances."

"I just saw in the news how an implant ruptured inside the chest of this one Turkish actress. The whole thing collapsed."

Yau Ying looked frightened. "Really?"

"Besides, even if you do get surgery, you can't hide it from Daihoi. If he loves you, he's not going to want you to take such a dangerous risk. Even if your bust is a little on the small side, what's the big deal? Like they say, bigger isn't always better. And implants don't necessarily look beautiful. I've seen a few customers who've had surgery, and when I accidentally brushed up against their breasts, I realized they were hard. They don't feel real at all."

Yau Ying seemed to take my words to heart. Laughing, she said, "It was just a thought. I don't really have the courage to go through with it."

Just then, Chui Yuk returned from the restroom.

"Guess who I just ran into?"

"Who?"

"Sissy Wong. She used to be a model, too. You've met her." I remembered Sissy Wong being a rather well-known fashion model whose claim to fame was that she was flat-chested.

"So it turns out that she got married," Chui Yuk said.

"Did she marry well?" I asked Chui Yuk.

"Her husband is a very highly regarded plastic surgeon. Lots of celebrities go to him. She gave me his business card."

Yau Ying's face lit up. Chui Yuk had no idea what she'd gotten herself into.

"A plastic surgeon? And he's highly regarded?" Yau Ying took the business card from Chui Yuk's hands.

"Sissy Wong looks like she's had breast implants herself. She used to be totally flat-chested, but now she's quite well-endowed," Chui Yuk said.

"Can I have this?" Yau Ying asked Chui Yuk.

"You want to have surgery?" Chui Yuk asked.

"You're not serious, are you?" I asked.

A few days later, I called Yau Ying.

"Please don't go through with the plastic surgery," I pleaded.

"I thought about it all night, and I still couldn't muster up the courage. You're so lucky. You don't have to go through this kind of mental strife," Yau Ying said.

"I have my own mental strife to deal with," I said.

"Do you want to meet Daihoi?" Yau Ying asked me.

"Can I?"

"Why wouldn't you? I've already told you all about him!"

Yau Ying planned to meet me for lunch in Central. When Daihoi appeared, he didn't strike me as the type who liked big-breasted women. He was about five foot ten and had finely chiseled features. When Yau Ying had told me he liked big breasts, I had imagined that he'd look sleazy. But that wasn't the case at all.

Daihoi was a criminal defense lawyer, and we started talking about a recent case of his.

"Remember the case where a woman dismembered her husband? Daihoi represented her," Yau Ying said.

"I only handled her case in the initial stages. One of the partners represented her when the case went to trial," Daihoi corrected her.

"She dismembered her own husband, then cooked and ate him. Yet she only got six years in prison. Don't you think that sentence was too lenient?" I asked Daihoi.

"Lawyers don't pass judgment on whether a certain person did a certain thing. They show whether there are reasonable grounds to believe that person did that thing. That woman was mentally disturbed," Daihoi said.

"She and her husband didn't sleep together for twenty years," Yau Ying said.

"Isn't it agonizing to defend someone and deny their actions if you know full well they're guilty?" I asked Daihoi.

"The entire legal profession is more or less agonizing," Daihoi said.

"I've heard that divorce is an agonizing ordeal, or something to that effect," I said.

"Not being able to get married in the first place is an agonizing ordeal, too." Yau Ying suddenly piped up, casting a bitter glance towards Daihoi.

Daihoi seemed completely deaf to her words.

"Being human is an agonizing ordeal," I joked.

"Ah! True, true," Yau Ying nodded vigorously.

When Yau Ying laughed, she accidentally spilled a few drops of lemonade onto her clothes. Daihoi took out his handkerchief and blotted up the stain. Daihoi seemed rather attentive to her needs. It was just that most men didn't want to get married.

"Would your wife ever turn you into minced meat sauce in your sleep?" I asked Sam over the phone when I got back to the shop.

"It's bound to happen sooner or later," Sam said.

"She must love you intensely, if she'd even think of devouring your flesh."

"Hating my guts would produce the same outcome."

"So there's no love, only hate?" I asked, feeling anguished.

"Would you ever turn me into minced meat sauce?" Sam asked me.

"I don't like minced meat sauce," I said.

"But if such an unfortunate turn of events were to occur, would you even be able to recognize that it was me?" Sam asked.

I suddenly felt petrified. The thought that this woman might actually turn him into minced meat sauce horrified me.

"Let's not talk about this anymore!"

"That might be the fate of a man who's unfaithful—not just to be made into minced meat sauce but to have his whole body made into minced meat sauce."

"Can we not talk about this anymore? Please?" I begged him.

"If you find out that I've been turned into minced meat sauce, don't worry. That was the price of loving you."

I couldn't hold back my tears. If he were going to be turned into minced meat sauce because of me, I'd rather give him back to the other woman.

That evening at my fashion design class, I thought so much about minced meat sauce that I lost my appetite. When Chen Dingleung invited me to join him for dinner after class, I didn't have the heart to turn him down, though. He picked a nearby Italian restaurant.

When he ordered the pasta with meat ragout, I almost threw up. I could hardly watch as he eagerly devoured it.

"I ran into my ex-wife yesterday," Chen Dingleung said.

"The two of you must really be karmically intertwined," I said.

"She's pregnant. She already has a bit of a baby bump." Chen Dingleung gestured with his hands.

"Does that make you happy or sad?" I couldn't tell from his expression.

"Both. We were together for five years, and we never were able to conceive. She hasn't been with her new husband for very long, and she's already pregnant." He laughed bitterly.

"Do you like children?"

"No, I don't. The idea of them scares me."

"So what do you have to be jealous of?"

"She's having someone else's child!"

"It's something you couldn't have, so you never imagined that someone else actually could. Isn't that so?"

"You're not like that?" He shot the question back at me.

"I've never experienced anything like that," I said.

"You sell lingerie, don't you?" he asked.

"Are you thinking of buying some as a gift?"

"Is there such a thing as lingerie designed for pregnant women?"

"Yes, there is. Because their bellies are so big, they can't get regular panties on anymore. Plus most pregnant women have to move up to a bigger bra size because their breasts swell up and their old bras don't fit anymore. After childbirth, the pressure in their chests subsides, so you have to use bras made of firmer material. And after giving birth, new moms have belly flab, which they can get rid of by wearing a postpartum girdle. Pregnant customers just mean more business for us," I said.

"I didn't know that being a woman was such hard work."

"Why are you so interested in pregnant women? Do you still think about your ex-wife all the time?"

"No, it's just that I felt strange when I saw her pregnant. I knew her body so well when we were married. If something about her body changed, I'd be curious as well as concerned."

"Is this how men think? After you split up, you still long for her body?"

"A man doesn't long for every woman's body," Chen Dingleung said. "Even if a man didn't love a woman, he can still remember her body, as long as her body made him happy."

"If what you're saying is true, then men can remember sex without love," I said.

"Are you saying that women aren't the same way?"

"Women need love in order to remember," I said.

"You're kidding!" He laughed coldly.

"Why do you think I'm kidding?"

"How can a woman only remember sexual relationships with certain men?"

"Because she loves that man," I said emphatically.

"Memories of sexual relationships are what they are. There's nothing more to them."

Chen Dingleung was scaring me. He was so self-assured, so convinced that he understood women perfectly. Of course a woman would remember only certain sexual relationships. But for a woman to admit such a thing was clearly too much for him to handle.

"A woman told me so," Chen Dingleung said.

"She told you that she remembered her sexual relationship with you, but that she didn't love you?"

"You love poking fun at people, don't you?"

"It's my forte."

Chen Dingleung drove me home in his jeep.

"When's Yu Mogwo's second book coming out? I promised I'd design the cover for him," said Chen Dingleung.

"He's doing a short study abroad program in the States. He and Chui Yuk were having problems, but now it looks like things are going to be OK."

"What kind of problems?" he asked me.

"The kind of problems all couples have!"

"What's this nonsense you speak of?" Chen Dingleung said, laughing.

"Is it fun driving a jeep?" I saw that he looked euphoric.

"Do you have a driver's license?" he asked me.

"I do. I took the driver's test five years ago, but I haven't driven since."

"Do you want to try driving this thing?"

"No, I haven't been behind the wheel in years."

"You're licensed—there's nothing to worry about!" Chen Dingleung said as he pulled over to the side of the road. "C'mon. It's your turn to drive."

"No!"

"C'mon! Don't worry. I'll be sitting right beside you."

Gathering all my courage, I climbed into the driver's seat.

"Do you still remember how to drive?" Chen Dingleung asked me.

I nodded.

"Great! Let's go!"

I started the engine, and off we went.

"Hey, not bad!" he said. "You can go a little faster."

I accelerated, and we sped down the highway. I don't quite know what happened next, but the jeep suddenly swerved off the road, and Chen Dingleung and I found ourselves roughly bumping along the shoulder. As we lurched to a stop, my skirt flew up over my legs and Chen Dingleung saw everything—probably even my underpants. I was mortified. I didn't know what I thought of this guy—the last thing I needed was him knowing what kind of underwear I wore.

"Are you OK?" he asked.

I gave a small nod as I hurriedly pulled my skirt back down, unable to look him in the eye.

"It's a miracle we didn't flip over. How about if I do the driving from now on?" he said, getting out of the car to walk to the driver's side.

"Did you know we have the same birthday?" I said, desperate to change the subject from my bad driving and my clothing mishap. I didn't want to hear a word about either one.

"We have the same birthday?"

"Yes! November third."

"That's a coincidence," he said, starting up the car.

When we arrived at my place, I thanked him for the ride and offered to pay for the damage.

"As long as it starts up, I'm not taking it to the shop. This car has always been covered in scars, just like me." He laughed sardonically.

"Well, see you later," I said.

"I hate to leave you so soon." With those words, he started up the engine and drove off. I didn't have a chance to see his expression, but he probably wanted to see my expression even less. The boldness of his words took me by complete surprise.

When I got inside, I took a look at myself in the mirror. I was in an unusually good mood. As it turned out, a woman needed to be admired. Only then did I realize my necklace was missing. I didn't have Chen

Dingleung's pager number, so I went and scoured the street outside. Just when I was about to head back inside, Chen Dingleung pulled up in his jeep.

"Looking for this?" He lowered the window and extended his hand. He was holding my scorpion necklace.

"Oh! Thank you." I grabbed it back.

"I found it inside the car," he said.

"Thanks again. See you later," I told him.

"See you," he said.

He still hadn't started the car by the time I stepped back into the building.

"Aren't you leaving?" I asked.

At that very moment—as if he were snapping awake—he abruptly waved good-bye. I felt uncertain about how I should have handled that. I had no intention of inviting Chen Dingleung up to my place. And yet I still felt bad. It turned out that rejecting someone was really hard. Maybe he didn't love me, and he was just longing for a woman's affection this evening, and I just happened to be a woman who sold lingerie, and he'd wrongly assumed that women who sold lingerie were loose, and therefore he thought he'd try to see if I'd sleep with him.

I called Chui Yuk. I wanted to see what she thought, but she piped up first. "Yu Mogwo is back. In fact, he's right beside me. I want him to talk to you."

"Chow Jeoi, how are you?" Yu Mogwo asked, sounding cheerful.

"I'm great. How are you? Did you just get back?" I asked him.

"I couldn't stop thinking about Chui Yuk," he said bluntly.

Chui Yuk then got back on the line. "He didn't say a word to me about coming back. I was shocked when he showed up at the door. We're going out for a midnight snack. Do you want to join us?"

"No thanks. I don't want to get in the way of your reunion."

"What did you want to talk to me about?"

"It's nothing urgent. I'll talk to you tomorrow."

I felt overwhelmed by sadness when I hung up. It seemed so unfair that Chui Yuk and Yu Mogwo could be together so freely, while Sam and I couldn't. I had no choice but to believe that the love between Sam and me—compared to the kind between Chui Yuk and Yu Mogwo, and even compared to whatever other love was out there in the world—was both profound and rare. That was the only way that I could endure the pain of knowing that we could never get married.

As I rinsed the scorpion necklace in warm water, I thought that if I were a scorpion, I might be fierce enough to steal Sam right from under that woman's nose. But that wasn't really an option. A truly righteous woman would never be the other woman in the first place.

The following evening, Chui Yuk invited me to dinner. She said Yu Mogwo wanted to thank me for taking care of her. Yu Mogwo looked much healthier than he had before he left for the States. In fact, he looked like his old self again. His fashion sense hadn't evolved much—he was still wearing sneakers. He didn't seem like he was on the brink of insanity anymore, which was fortunate.

"Chow Jeoi wants to know how hummingbirds can fly backwards," Chui Yuk said.

"It turns out hummingbird wings are rather unusual," Yu Mogwo said.

"How so?" I asked him.

"The wings of hummingbirds move at a rate faster than fifty times per second. As a result, they can hold their position in midair and move either forwards or backwards. It turns out they can travel at a speed of thirty to thirty-eight miles an hour, while a sparrow can go only twelve to eighteen miles an hour."

"I had no idea," I said.

"But it's not very useful to be able to fly backwards," Yu Mogwo said.

"Why not?" Chui Yuk asked.

"Human beings don't have much use for walking backwards. If you think of a place you want to go back to, all you have to do is just turn around and walk there," Yu Mogwo said.

"When people can't go back to a place where they used to be, their thoughts can go back. It's just their bodies that can't," I said.

"I'd rather not be able to fly backwards," Chui Yuk said, laying her hand on Yu Mogwo's thigh. "Wouldn't it be scary if Yu Mogwo went back to the way he was before he went to the States?"

"You were pretty frightening," I told Yu Mogwo.

He chuckled.

"I don't think there are any hummingbirds in Hong Kong," I said.

"Most hummingbirds live in the Americas. There are roughly three hundred species in all," Yu Mogwo said.

"Do you have a sample specimen?" I asked him.

"Are you looking for one?" he asked.

"Why are you so interested in hummingbirds?" Chui Yuk asked.

"Because they're singular in this world," I said.

"I have a friend I met in the States who does a lot of research on birds. I can try asking him," Yu Mogwo said.

"Thanks. Have you ever thought about writing a story involving hummingbirds?" I asked him.

"A science-fiction story?"

"Like where a man turns into a hummingbird and he flies backwards, all the way back into the past, and marries the woman that he could never marry before . . . ," I said.

4

Grade A in a Lover's Eyes

Sam and I were eating at my apartment when I noticed that he was wearing a watch I'd never seen before. It made me uneasy. Sam noticed that I was staring at his watch.

"I bought it myself," he said.

"I wasn't asking," I said, feigning ignorance.

"But you've been staring at my watch throughout dinner."

"Oh, was I?"

"I bought it more than ten years ago. I dug it out recently and started wearing it."

"Oh, yeah?" I pretended not to care.

"Weren't you wondering who gave it to me?"

"I don't know."

"You're the only woman who gives me gifts," he said, putting his hands on my shoulders. But I suddenly felt sad, since I wasn't the only woman in his life. Even a wristwatch could trigger a flood of thoughts that I couldn't let go of.

"I didn't mean to stare at your watch," I said, as tears welled in my eyes.

"Don't cry." Sam brushed away my tears. "Why is it that you always cry at the happiest moments? We're together right now. Aren't you supposed to be happy right now?" Sam asked me sadly.

"Maybe you're right. But it's hard to be happy when I never know when or if I'll see you again," I said.

"You will unless I die," he said.

"I just want to ask you this one time. Are you ever going to get a divorce?" I hadn't expected to have the nerve to ask him that.

He didn't answer me.

Yau Ying called me at three in the morning.

"You're not asleep, are you?" she asked me.

"I can't fall asleep," I said.

"Why not?"

Maybe because I needed so badly to be comforted—and because Yau Ying was my childhood friend—I told her about what was going on between Sam and me.

"I never would have imagined . . . ," she said despondently.

"You never would have imagined that I'd be the other woman?"

"I never imagined that you'd go on to become a typical housewife and mother, but I didn't think you'd become the other woman, either. You were always such an independent girl."

"It's because I was so independent that I ended up becoming the other woman! That's what made me able to handle being alone. If I could be a little more dependent, then I'd make a good wife," I said.

"So am I more of a good wife or the other woman?" Yau Ying asked.

"For you, it's hard to say. But by the looks of it, you're more of a good wife—the future wife of a lawyer. What about Daihoi? Where is he?"

"He's in the bedroom sleeping. I'm calling you from the kitchen."

"The kitchen?"

"I couldn't get to sleep, so I came in here to get something to eat. But then I wasn't hungry, and I felt like calling you instead." Yau Ying was clearly worried about something.

"What's the matter?" I asked her.

"I smelled someone else's perfume inside Daihoi's car."

"Someone else's perfume?"

"I use Chanel No. 5. This fragrance smelled like Dior."

"What did you do?"

"I asked him which scent he preferred," Yau Ying said, suddenly roaring with laughter.

"You had the nerve to do that?"

"I'm surprised myself that I could be so matter-of-fact about it. I wonder if it means I don't love him anymore."

"How did Daihoi answer?"

"He said he didn't know what I was talking about."

"Does Olivia Wu use Dior?"

"No, she wears Issey Miyake."

"So maybe Daihoi dropped off a female colleague on the way home, and she happened to be wearing Dior."

"That's what I told myself to make myself feel better."

"Your nose can be sensitive to a fault, you know," I said.

"I know! If I hadn't smelled that perfume, I would be sound asleep right now."

"You don't know how much I envy you. At least you and Daihoi can live together. You should be grateful and not so suspicious of him."

"If you and Tong Man Sam could live together, you'd be suspicious of him sometimes, too," Yau Ying said.

Maybe Yau Ying was right. I'd always wanted to be able to live with Sam. It hadn't ever occurred to me that the reason we were in love now—and that we could continue to love each other so deeply—was precisely because we couldn't live together. If we were to see each other day in and day out, life might very well become a series of troublesome spats.

"Why haven't the two of you gotten married? If you were married, you might feel a little more at ease," I said.

"He brought it up a long time ago, but hasn't mentioned it even once in the past two years. He won't—and I won't, either. A lot of people probably think I'm being foolish, since we've been together for seven years. But I don't like to tell people off. I just want him to marry me if and when he wants to, not because otherwise he'll be the reason I've squandered years of my life. There's a big difference between those two things. Besides, I don't seem to love him the way I used to."

"You don't feel any anxiety about your future with him?"

"Maybe we've gotten so used to living together that neither of us want to change the way we are to suit someone new."

"I think you may love him more now," I said.

"What makes you say that?"

"Because the more you love someone, the more afraid you are of losing them. It's hard to deal with that kind of pressure, so you tell yourself you don't really love him that much. That way, in case you do lose him, you won't be as hurt."

She was silent.

"Am I wrong?" I asked.

She let out a deep sigh, and said, "I'm just a secretary. Even if I work my hardest, I'm still just a secretary. I don't have much of a career, whereas Daihoi is in the prime of his. I'm not jealous—there shouldn't be jealousy between two people who are close—but I just feel like I have no security whatsoever. He's like a ray of light, and I'm nearing a dead end."

I finally understood why Yau Ying was unhappy. It terrified her that there was such a chasm between their job situations. But I didn't know what to say to console her.

***

Three days later, Daihoi showed up at the lingerie store. It seemed odd to me that he was there.

"I want to buy a gift for Yau Ying," Daihoi said. "She's been buying a lot of designer lingerie recently, so I figure she really likes it."

"I'll gather some nice pieces for you to choose from."

I picked out a few silk negligees, and he chose a pink one. If Daihoi demonstrated any lawyerlike quality, it was the quality of judiciousness.

"How's Yau Ying?" I asked him.

"She's meeting a friend for lunch. Are you free? Would you like to grab lunch?" Daihoi asked me.

"Aren't you worried that Yau Ying might get the wrong idea?" I said, laughing.

"She doesn't get jealous."

He didn't have any idea that she'd become jealous to the point where it was a serious problem. But I figured there was no harm in accepting his invitation and agreed to go.

"Has Yau Ying seemed worried lately?" Daihoi asked me once we were seated.

"I can't really tell." I didn't want to talk to him about what was going on with her.

At the end of lunch, Daihoi lit a cigarette. He leaned back in his chair and said, "I really love her."

I found it strange that Daihoi announced his love for Yau Ying to me like that. But it's always moving when a man is so frank as to openly declare his love for his girlfriend. Maybe there was no need for Yau Ying to have been so unhappy recently, I thought. In spite of the fact that they had been together for seven years, it seemed as if they didn't understand one another. He didn't know she was jealous. She didn't know that he loved her. How on earth did these two people communicate?

"Why are you telling me this?" I asked him.

"You two were good friends as children. She's never had many friends," Daihoi said.

"Do you want me to tell her what you said?"

Daihoi shook his head. "I have the courage to tell you that I love her, but I don't have the courage to tell her."

"Why not?"

"She's the kind of woman who makes it hard to tell her that you love her."

This was the first time I'd ever heard of a woman who made it impossible for the man who loved her to show it.

"Are you saying that she doesn't think she's worthy of being loved?"

"No." Daihoi looked like he was mulling over how to express his thoughts. Ever the lawyer, he was probably carefully choosing his words, as if he were in court, in order to be as accurate as possible.

"It's like with some lawyers, you don't tell them the truth because you can never tell what they're thinking. You can't tell if they even believe you," Daihoi eventually said.

"You don't think she'll believe that you love her?"

"It's almost as if she doesn't cherish me."

"From what I understand, she cherishes you a lot," I said. If Daihoi had known that Yau Ying considered getting breast implants for him, he'd never again say that she didn't cherish him.

"Does she seem like that to you?" he asked.

"All I know is that you both seem to cherish each other."

"But it never seems like she cares," Daihoi said.

Finally, I understood. Daihoi was probably talking about the business with the perfume.

"Are you talking about how there was the scent of perfume in your car, but instead of asking you about it, she asked you which fragrance you liked better?"

"She told you?"

"Uh-huh."

"Don't you think she acts differently from most other women?" Daihoi asked.

"So then who left the scent of perfume in your car?"

"I dropped off a female prosecutor on the way home."

I'd guessed correctly.

"Jealousy doesn't always show," I said. You couldn't tell by the look on Yau Ying's face that she was jealous, yet her fear had alerted Daihoi to the fact that she indeed was.

"It's also hard to let someone know that you're jealous." Daihoi laughed darkly.

I'd always believed that as long as two people really loved each other, things would work out between them. But apparently that wasn't the case. Some people could love someone in their heart but not know how to express it.

As Daihoi and I crossed a pedestrian bridge on our way back to work, a man carrying several bundles of brightly colored silks passed by us. He abruptly stopped right in front of me. It was Chen Dingleung.

"What are you doing here?" I asked.

Chen Dingleung sounded a bit embarrassed when he replied. He probably assumed that Daihoi was my boyfriend, and was therefore hesitant about whether to call out to me.

"I have to run—I've got to get back to work," Daihoi told me.

"Where are you off to?" I asked Chen Dingleung.

"Was that your boyfriend?" he asked.

I chuckled, but didn't answer his question. I didn't think there was any need for me to tell Chen Dingleung the truth. If he wanted to jump to conclusions, then let him. Moreover, it could be fun to play him off against Daihoi.

"Those are beautiful fabrics," I said, touching one of the fabrics in his arms. "Looks comfortable."

"It is. It's very high-quality material. I'm working on my own designs and setting up my own brand."

"Congratulations," I said. "Where are you heading? I can help you carry some of that."

"Thanks. Careful, though. It's really heavy!" Chen Dingleung said as he placed one of the bundles into my hands.

"Wow . . . you're really unloading this thing on me?" I teased.

"If a man can do the job, so can a woman," he said as he began to walk.

"Where are we going?" I asked, following him.

"We're almost there." He entered a shopping center, and stopped in front of a tiny shop space.

"This is your store?" I felt like it didn't suit him at all.

"My old office had a view of the sea. This office has a view of a shopping center," he said, chuckling to himself.

"You didn't mention this big project of yours the last time we spoke," I said.

"That guy just now wasn't your boyfriend," Chen Dingleung said, taking the bundle of fabric out of my hands.

"How do you know?"

"The look in your eyes says you two aren't lovers."

"Not every pair of lovers has the same look in their eyes. He's my friend's boyfriend. Are you the only one here?"

"I have a partner."

"Should I patronize your shop and have something made to help you kick off your new venture?" I asked.

"Of course you're welcome to. What kind of piece are you interested in?"

"I don't know off the top of my head."

"I know what you'd look good in."

"Oh? What would I look good in?"

"You'll know what I mean when you see it."

"When will it be ready?" I asked.

"When it's finished, I'll let you know."

"Is this how you plan to treat all your customers?"

"I plan to give them a pickup date."

"How come I'm not getting one?"

"That might just be because I'm going to work extra hard on yours. So don't ask me when it'll be ready."

That evening, I had dinner with Chui Yuk and Yau Ying.

"Daihoi came to see me today," I told Yau Ying.

Yau Ying looked stunned. "Why?"

"He told me that he really loves you."

Yau Ying's expression went from stunned to sweet.

"Why would he tell you that?" Yau Ying asked.

"Because if he told you, you wouldn't believe him. He didn't say that I should tell you. In fact, I promised him I wouldn't."

"He's never told me that before," Yau Ying said.

"You've never told him that you love him, either—isn't that right?"

Yau Ying was silent.

"You've never told him that you love him?" Chui Yuk said. "You've been together for seven years!"

"I don't know how to say it," Yau Ying said.

"I tell Yu Mogwo that I love him all the time."

"But it's so hard to say those words," Yau Ying insisted. "I've never told any man that I loved him."

"Daihoi really wants to hear you say them," I said.

"Really? Then why doesn't he say them first?"

If they each were waiting for the other to say those words first, then they were both going to be on their deathbeds before anyone said anything. I'd never dream of being so stingy with those words.

"You're afraid to lose," I told Yau Ying. "If you tell him that you love him first, then he'll know that you really love him. If you love him more than he loves you, it'll be like you're losing. That's what you're thinking, isn't it?" I said.

"That's how men are, right? If you tell him you love him, he won't tell you that he loves you," Yau Ying said.

"Why not?" Chui Yuk said.

"If a man knows that you love him, he won't bother to say that he loves you because he already has the upper hand. Men only say 'I love you' when they lack confidence," Yau Ying said.

I'd forgotten that Yau Ying was the kind of person who was afraid to lose. When we were little, she refused to compete with me at jumping rope because she knew she wouldn't win.

"Because you don't want to lose, you also don't want him to know that you're jealous, isn't that right?"

"Why'd you have to tell him that I'm jealous? Daihoi doesn't like women who are jealous," Yau Ying said.

"He thought you didn't cherish him because you weren't jealous," I said.

"He said that I didn't cherish him?" Yau Ying said, sounding angry.

"Men aren't as sensitive as women. He doesn't know the pain that it's causing you," I said.

"Why does it seem like you and Daihoi are at war, and you're both wearing all this armor?" Chui Yuk said.

"We've been doing it that way for seven years, and things have been fine!"

I was starting to worry about Yau Ying and Daihoi. Neither one was willing to let the other have the upper hand. That kind of relationship could be dangerous.

The phone was ringing when I got home that night. It was Sam.

"Where are you?" I asked him.

"At the office."

"If I told you right now that I loved you, would you feel like you had the upper hand?" I asked him.

"How would I?"

"You really wouldn't?"

"If you don't believe me, why don't you tell me right now that you love me?"

"No way. Why don't you say it first?"

"There are other people around me!" he said.

"So why did you call me?"

"Because I miss you."

That night, those words—"I miss you"—seemed especially warm and touching. We were better off than Yau Ying and Daihoi. They might live together, but each of them was consumed by their own separate worries. When I had something on my mind, Sam knew. The only thing I didn't know was how he really felt about his wife.

"When you say that you miss me, I start gloating. Right now you're losing," I teased him.

"I'm always losing." The way he said it was eerily heartbreaking.

"If I let you be the one who calls the shots, would you still say that you're losing?"

"You can leave me anytime you want," he said.

"You can leave me anytime you want, too. I'm just a passing traveler who crosses paths with you during your lifetime," I said sadly.

"I've never treated you like a passing traveler."

I knew that, but I nonetheless felt that way. In my early twenties, I'd never understood how important the social status of being married was for a woman. Then I met Sam. Sharing a love wasn't enough. I started to understand why some women clung to their marital status, refusing to let go of it even after the love was gone. They protected it fiercely, hoping he'd come running back to them one day. Perhaps the greatest sin a man could commit towards the woman he truly loved was to deny her social recognition of their relationship—and if he were in a marriage he couldn't leave, he'd try to show her all the love he could to atone for it.

"Do you love me because you feel guilty? You shouldn't feel guilty. I only have myself to blame," I said.

"If you don't love someone, why would you feel guilty about it?" Sam said.

When Sam hung up, I took a hot bath. Afterwards I couldn't get to sleep. Sam said that if you didn't love someone, you didn't feel guilty about it. So if there had once been love, wasn't there guilt, too? Did he feel guilt towards his wife, since he'd once loved her?

Around three in the morning, the scent of cake started to waft up from downstairs. Ms. Kwok usually started baking around seven, so I wondered why I smelled it at this hour. I got dressed and went downstairs.

I knocked on the door of the cake shop, and Ms. Kwok came and unlocked the door. She looked haggard, and her red lipstick had worn off.

"Ms. Chow, why haven't you gone to bed yet?" she asked me.

"I can't fall asleep. Plus I smelled cake," I said.

"I'm so sorry. I shouldn't be baking at this hour, but I don't know what else to do with myself. I can't sleep, either." She seemed to have a lot on her mind. "Why don't you come in and have a cup of tea? The cake is just about ready!"

"All right," I said. The smell was so enticing. "Is this a cake someone ordered?"

"No, it's something I'm making for myself. Come have a look."

She led me into the kitchen and pulled a gorgeous mango cake out of the oven.

She served me a slice. I took a bite. It was delicious.

"Ms. Kwok, this cake tastes incredible."

"Don't call me Ms. Kwok. My friends call me Kwok Seon."

"Seon? Seon as in bamboo shoot?"

"My father loved eating bamboo shoots, so he named me after them."

"Kwok Seon is a really unique name."

"The wonderful thing about bamboo shoots is that you can get them year-round. I love eating them myself."

"How'd you get into the business of selling cakes?"

"I learned from my mother. She was a housewife and a very talented cook. She was known far and wide for her cakes. I'm still not as good as she was. When I was eighteen, I got married and moved from Indonesia here to Hong Kong. I had a son, then a daughter, and I worked the whole time I raised them. I couldn't get used to eating Hong Kong cakes, and suddenly the idea came to me: I'd bake and sell my own cakes. But running your own shop is such hard work! It turns out that just being a wife is a much more comfortable life." Kwok Seon rubbed her shoulder with her hand.

"Let me help you." Standing behind her, I massaged her shoulders.

"Why, thank you."

"Is your husband against the idea of you working?"

"We're divorced."

"I'm sorry to hear that."

"Not at all. My marriage gave me not only a son and a daughter but also a generous alimony. Even if I never work again, I won't ever have to worry about my retirement."

"What about your son and daughter?"

"My son is in England, and my daughter is in the States. They're both grown up now."

"It's too bad they're not here to eat your cakes."

"Do you know why I got divorced?" Kwok Seon asked me.

"Was it because there was another woman?"

Kwok Seon nodded. "She was twenty years younger than my husband. The first time I saw her, I was startled. She looked just like me. The only difference was that she was a younger version. The thought that my husband was in love with her was surprisingly comforting. It was proof that he'd once loved me deeply, since he'd gone and found someone who looked just like me."

Did I look like Sam's wife? That was something I'd always wondered about and hoped to find out someday.

"I cut quite a charming figure when I was younger!" Kwok Seon was growing nostalgic.

"I can imagine."

"I used to have a waist," she said.

I nearly sprayed out a mouthful of tea. Kwok Seon's words, which were so sincere, were also completely hilarious. I was about to hide a smile, but Kwok Seon herself was grinning.

"It's true." She stood up and put her hands on her hips. "Before I got married, my waistline was twenty-five inches. After my first child was born, it was twenty-nine inches. After my second child, well, that's when things really went downhill."

"I've never had a twenty-five-inch waistline. Even at my thinnest, I was only around twenty-seven inches," I said.

Kwok Seon pinched her love handles. "My waist is like something from the distant past. Now that it's gone, it's not coming back."

"Believe me, your waist is not that thick." I estimated her waist to be about thirty-three inches.

"You really think so?" Kwok asked me.

"You have a very shapely bust, which makes your waistline look narrow. You're lucky that way."

I imagined that she must have been quite a stunner back in the day.

"My bust? Let's not even go there. I'm drooping all the way down to my waist. The way I look now, it's a travesty." Kwok Seon let out a bitter laugh.

I didn't quite know how to respond to her honesty.

"After I got divorced, I went through two boyfriends. But I jumped ship when things reached that pivotal moment," Kwok Seon said.

"That pivotal moment?"

"When we were about to become intimate. I broke up with them before we got intimate."

"How come?"

"I was afraid to let them see my flabby figure. I was afraid they'd run. Just this evening, there was a man who ran," Kwok Seon said dejectedly.

"Hold on a second. I'll be right back . . ."

I sprinted upstairs to my apartment and grabbed one of my business cards, then went back down to the cake shop.

"Here's my business card. Come see me tomorrow."

Sure enough, Kwok Seon walked into the lingerie shop the following afternoon. Kwok Seon's figure wasn't nearly as terrible as she'd made it out to be. Her skin was smooth and pale—a rare quality in someone her age—and she wore a perfectly respectable size. Her breasts did sag a bit, but not all the way down to her waist.

"I used to be flatter," Kwok Seon said.

So bigger breasts weren't necessarily such a pleasant thing.

The waist problem was easy enough to solve. With the aid of a corset, she could narrow it by three inches.

I soon discovered that Kwok Seon's biggest problem was the flab around her belly, which was full of wrinkles. When Kwok Seon turned left, the belly flab also turned left, and when she turned right, it also turned right. When she bowed, so did the belly flab.

"I'd seriously cut off my belly flab if I could," Kwok Seon said angrily.

I had Kwok Seon try on a new bra, corset, and shaping shorts. Fastening her corset all the way up was no easy task.

"This ensemble is going to pull it in as much as possible. You can wear it on special occasions or under something that's slim fitting. For everyday wear, there are looser-fitting ones," I said.

Kwok Seon scrutinized herself in the mirror. At that moment, she had a 36-27-36 figure.

"It's a miracle!" Kwok Seon gushed as she gazed at herself in the mirror. "How can this be possible?"

"It's all the work of wires and elastic," I said.

"Elastic and wire are truly great inventions!" Kwok Seon cried out.

"This woman you see with the stunning figure is actually made of heaps of wires," Kwok Seon said as she paid for her purchases.

"I'll be waiting for good news from you," I said.

That evening was the last class in my fashion design course, and the dozen or so students in the class had organized a dinner for Chen Dingleung. After dinner, we all headed over to a dance club. Some people in the group clamored for Chen Dingleung to sing a song.

"The only song I know is 'I Will Wait for You,'" Chen Dingleung said, flashing a grin my way.

"They probably don't have that song," I said.

"In that case, let's dance—if I may have that honor," he said to me.

So we hit the dance floor. Chen Dingleung wasn't much of a dancer. He just sort of swayed his body in time to the music.

"You don't dance much, do you?" I said.

He took my hand and pulled me to the center of the dance floor before letting go.

"Do two people with the same birthday have any chance of becoming lovers?" he asked.

If it weren't for Sam, maybe I'd have given Chen Dingleung a chance. But I wasn't about to cheat on Sam. If one of us was going to cheat, I'd rather have it be him.

"People with the same birthday don't necessarily become lovers. Most people don't have the same birthday as their lovers," I said.

"They just don't have many opportunities to meet someone else with the same birthday, that's all. The probability of two people having the same birthday is one in three hundred sixty-five," Chen Dingleung said.

"Well, this really must be fate, then!" I said. "I just hope we don't die on the same day."

Chen Dingleung was annoying me so much that I didn't know what else to say.

"You said you were going to design the cover of Yu Mogwo's next book. He's back now," I said, changing the subject.

"Oh, really? You should have him get in touch with me," Chen Dingleung said.

"What about my new piece? When's it going to be ready?"

"I haven't started yet. I told you not to rush me."

As soon as I changed the subject, he seemed to lose interest. He never made his intentions clear, and I never told him that I had a boyfriend. Sam was special to me. I didn't want to talk about him. I had a strange fear that someone might know one of Sam's relatives or his wife's relatives and tell them about Sam and me. I knew the chances of that happening were slim, but I still didn't want to risk it.

Chen Dingleung led two other women from the class out to the dance floor. He looked like he was having a good time with them, and I wondered whether it was a move aimed at making me jealous. It didn't work, though. Why would I feel jealous, since I knew perfectly well that he wasn't interested in them?

As we all left the club, someone suggested going to get a late-night snack.

"I have to work in the morning. I can't go," I said.

"I can't go, either," Chen Dingleung said, looking over at me with deep sincerity in his eyes.

I suddenly felt terrified. I saw a taxi coming and ran to catch it.

I jumped into the cab and avoided looking back at Chen Dingleung. He'd given me a ride home after almost every class, and I was worried he might have wanted to take me home tonight. He must have realized I was trying to get away from him when I dove into the taxi like that.

I only felt truly safe once I set foot inside my apartment. I wanted to call Sam and say, "There's a guy who likes me and is bent on pursuing me, and I'm scared." But I knew he was most likely at home, sleeping beside his wife at that hour.

I started to understand how people who are unfaithful are pitiful. They don't mean to be unfaithful; they're just afraid of being alone. It takes a lot of love to be loyal and accountable to another person. If I didn't have so much love in me, I'd never be able to handle the loneliness.

When Sam called me the next day, I didn't tell him what had happened the night before. I knew he wouldn't like the fact that I'd been getting rides home regularly from some other man who had shown a romantic interest in me.

On the first Wednesday evening in October, Sam brought over a bunch of giant crabs he'd bought.

"I don't know how to cook these," I said.

"Who says you're cooking? I'm going to cook them for you. You don't have to do a thing."

He jauntily went into the kitchen and started washing the crabs.

"Not so fast . . . ," I said.

"Why?"

"You need to put on an apron first."

I took out a red apron with lace trim and gave it to him. I'd bought it when I first moved in and only worn it a few times.

"That won't look too good on me, will it?"

"What are you worried about? I want you to wear it."

I couldn't help laughing at the sight of him in my apron. It was the first time I'd ever seen him in one. With that apron on, Sam looked like he was really, truly part of this household.

"You can't take off that apron tonight," I said, hugging him.

"What are you talking about? It looks so bizarre on me."

"I like you this way," I said, feeling audacious.

When the crabs were done, Sam removed the shells carefully and methodically. The golden roe oozed out.

"I'll pick out the meat for you. These parts aren't any good. You can't eat them." He picked up a chunk and tossed it in the garbage.

After we ate the roe, only the legs and claws remained. I didn't want to eat them.

"Why not?" he asked me.

"It's too much work!" I said.

Sam took out a tiny fork and started picking the meat out of a crab leg for me. He became so engrossed that he forgot about his own food.

"You don't have to do so much for me," I said.

"All I did was cook some crabs."

"Why did you choose this particular night to cook for me?"

"This afternoon I passed by a Chinese market and these crabs looked so good, I just had to buy some so we could enjoy them together. No special reason. What, you suspect I'm up to something?"

"In a month, I'll be thirty," I sobbed.

Thirty had always seemed a long ways off, but it was fast approaching. Shouldn't a woman assess her own needs when she turns thirty?

"You said you'd leave me when you turned thirty," he said.

"It'd be better if you left me," I said grimly.

"I can't do that. I'm never going to leave you."

"I hate you!" I snapped at him.

"Why?"

"Someday you're not going to want me anymore, and I'm going to be a fat old woman that nobody wants."

"You have a great figure. Just don't let yourself go after you're thirty, and you'll look terrific," Sam said, wrapping his arms around me.

I didn't know whether to laugh or cry. "Isn't it true that when my figure starts going downhill, you won't want me anymore?"

"By the time your figure goes downhill, I'll be an old man."

"If only that were true," I said, breaking free from his embrace.

"Tell me—what would you like for your birthday?"

"You already gave me this apartment."

"This apartment isn't a birthday present."

"If you can't be with me on that day, then I don't want anything—and I don't ever want to see you again," I told him.

"That's terrible!" He squeezed my hand.

"I couldn't be with you on your last birthday. I don't want to go through that again. I don't ever want to be stabbed in the heart like that again."

"I already said I'd spend your birthday with you, just as I have for the past three years. Now tell me, what do you want for your birthday?"

"I haven't really thought about it. Buy me whatever you want. I just want to be with you." I leaned over his shoulders. "I want to be lying in your arms when I turn thirty."

On November 2, Yau Ying and Chui Yuk invited me out for Japanese food to celebrate my birthday.

"Happy thirtieth!" Yau Ying said when she saw me.

"Please don't say the number thirty."

"I turned thirty three full months ago. I'm so glad it's your turn now!" Yau Ying said with sadistic delight.

"I still have one year and eight months to go." Chui Yuk was beaming.

They'd gotten Kwok Seon to make me a birthday cake in the shape of a bra.

"It's a 34B. Since you've been blessed with such abundance, we can only wish you eternal firmness!" Chui Yuk said.

"I wish you eternal firmness, too. You're carrying an even heavier load!"

"We still have an hour before midnight. Where do you guys want to go celebrate?" Chui Yuk asked.

"Anywhere is fine with me. I drove Daihoi's convertible here," Yau Ying said. Daihoi's German convertible was purple with a white top. The license plate number was AC8166.

"AC doesn't stand for A Cup, does it?" I asked.

"His father gave him this license plate. I've always thought AC stood for A Cup, too," Yau Ying said.

Chui Yuk hopped into the car. "32A, start your engine!"

Yau Ying got in the driver's seat and asked, "34B, where would you like to usher in your thirtieth birthday?"

"I want to go . . . I want to go somewhere that's a day behind Hong Kong time. Where I'll still be twenty-nine at midnight tonight," I said.

"I don't think there's a place a whole day behind Hong Kong time. There's nowhere more than eighteen hours behind us, which is what Hawaii is. And also French Polynesia," Chui Yuk said.

"Let's go to French Polynesia, then! I want to be eighteen hours younger!" I stood up inside the car and said, "It's practically dawn here."

"Believe me, being thirty isn't the worst thing in the world," Yau Ying said. "Being thirty and not having a man—now *that's* the worst thing in the world."

"I think having a thirty-three-inch waist is worse than being thirty and not having a man," Chui Yuk said.

When we arrived at the stunning beaches of Shek O, Chui Yuk asked to stop the car and ran into a little shop. She emerged a few minutes later with a bag and announced, "I just bought a few bottles of French mineral water. Close your eyes and imagine . . . we've arrived in French Polynesia. You're now eighteen hours younger!"

"Wonderful!" I said.

Would anyone on earth actually travel to another place just to be eighteen hours younger? Even if you did, you'd instantly be eighteen hours older when you returned home. Your happiness from the eighteen hours that you gained would be short lived.

At midnight, we celebrated in French Polynesia—or as close as I was going to get to it, anyway. There was no doubt about it: my thirtieth birthday had arrived.

"Doesn't Chen Dingleung have the same birthday as you?" Chui Yuk suddenly asked me. "Are you going to wish him a happy birthday?"

"He's probably out celebrating with other people."

"I bet he misses you," Yau Ying said.

"Don't remind him. He scares me," I said.

"You're too cruel to him," Chui Yuk said. "I'm worried he won't design the cover for Yu Mogwo's book, and he's almost done writing it."

"Fine, then! I'll keep stringing him along for your benefit," I said.

"I wish there were subdivisions to ages, like there are for bra sizes," Yau Ying said. "There could be three stages of development—30A, 30B, and 30C. They should just make thirty happen over three years instead."

"Then the goal would be to reach D," Chui Yuk said.

"What's Sam getting you for your birthday?" Yau Ying asked me.

"I'll find out tonight," I said.

"Sam treats you so well."

"Doesn't Daihoi treat you well?"

"How many men are there who'd buy an apartment for a woman, especially when that woman isn't even his wife? The law firm handles a lot of house deeds, and buying houses for girlfriends is virtually unheard of. Even if a man does buy one, he doesn't just fork over the whole sum in cash. They all pay in installments, so that they can stop making the payments if they break up. The ones that have real money make their mistresses live in these sprawling mansions under their company's name. Daihoi and I both have our names on the deed for our place."

"I'm really touched by it. Sam's no billionaire. He works his fingers to the bone to earn that kind of money. It comes from holding down a high-pressure job."

"What do you want in a man?" Yau Ying asked me.

"I want a man who's first-rate," I said. "He has to be Grade A."

"The man I have is Grade A," Chui Yuk said happily as she lay down on the beach.

"How would you rate Daihoi?" I asked Yau Ying.

"A minus."

"Why an A minus?" I asked Yau Ying.

"If there's such a thing as an A minus, then I want to give Yu Mogwo an A plus," Chui Yuk said.

"He hasn't asked me to marry him, so he only gets an A minus," Yau Ying said.

"If Sam weren't already married, I'd give him an A plus plus," I said, reclining in the sand.

"Are there any actual Grade-A men in this world?" Yau Ying asked.

"In the eyes of a lover, they're all Grade A!" I said.

"Why do you think Daihoi is Grade A?" Chui Yuk asked Yau Ying.

"Seven years ago, I saw him in court one day and fell in love on the spot. There was just this radiant glow about him. He was new to the law firm at the time, but I already knew he was an A," Yau Ying said.

"Grade-A men and A-cup women are like two peas in a pod," Chui Yuk said.

"Right. I don't want Grade B. I'd rather be alone than settle for a Grade-B man," I said.

"Do you know how much work it takes to get yourself a Grade A?" Yau Ying asked me.

"No pain, no gain," I said. "In order to get a Grade-A man, doesn't your appearance have to be at least a B?"

"Yes," Chui Yuk said. "If you go without a bra for a long time, your breasts will start to sag. Likewise, if you don't work hard to love a man, you'll lose him. You can't just take him for granted."

"No, there are women who seem like they don't have to lift a finger in order to get a good man. She'll always be the apple of his eye, even if she doesn't love him that much," Yau Ying said. "Then other women do everything in their power, and still don't get what they want."

"That's why you should consider yourself lucky if you actually manage to reap what you sow," I said.

"Don't you want to get married?" Yau Ying asked me.

"I do, but how can I?"

"So you're going to stay with him your whole life, without any name or status."

"That in itself is a form of commitment," I said.

Yau Ying and I clinked bottles. "Here's to your big commitment. Cheers!"

The three of us took our empty bottles and filled them with sand. We dug a deep hole along the beach and placed the bottles inside, then covered them up with sand.

"When you're forty, we'll come back and dig up these three bottles," Chui Yuk said.

"By that time, you might have to bring two kids. And because you just gave birth, your breasts will be even bigger than they are now!" I teased Chui Yuk.

"You'll still be committed to Sam!" Chui Yuk said.

"Is that a blessing or a curse?" I asked her.

"Forty years old. How scary is that!" Yau Ying covered her face.

"It doesn't matter how scared you are. The day will eventually come," I said.

"I'm going to snag a man who'll be with me when I turn forty, no matter what," Yau Ying said.

At 9 a.m. on November 3, there was a knock on my door. It was Kwok Seon, who stood there, holding a cake in the shape of a rose. "Happy birthday!" she cried.

"Who's it from?"

"It's from Mr. Tong."

Sam. I should've guessed.

"When did he order it?" I said as I took the cake into my hands.

"A week ago."

"And this is from me," Kwok Seon said as she took out an exquisite tin box and handed it to me.

I opened the lid to find a batch of cookies. I took a bite of one.

"Thank you. They're delicious."

"Your boyfriend obviously really loves you. When are the two of you getting married?"

"I'm never marrying him!" I said, making a face that suggested I didn't want to get married. "What about you? What's new with you?"

"Not much. Finding a boyfriend is much more difficult at my age than it is for you. But a few days ago, a friend of mine invited me to go to an alumni association ball. I might meet someone there, who knows?"

"Well, I wish you the best of luck!"

"I hope you have a lovely evening tonight."

After Kwok Seon left, Sam called.

"The cake is so beautiful!" I said. "Is it just a cake—no flowers?"

"You wanted flowers?"

"I want you to dress up as a flower and come see me," I said.

"Since when are there flowers that big? I'd make a better tree."

That evening, I got all dressed up and waited for my tree to show up. Sam had said he'd call me after work, and then he'd take me out for dinner. But he still hadn't called by eight o'clock. What on earth was he doing? At 9:40 p.m., the phone finally rang.

"Hello . . . ?" In my heart, I imagined the worst. Then again, if there'd been some kind of accident, he wouldn't have been able to call me.

"Where are you?" I asked him.

"I'm at the hospital."

"Why?" My heart fell into my stomach.

"Her father's in the hospital. It's a relapse of an old illness."

"Oh." I didn't believe him. "What a coincidence."

I was desperately hoping that he'd give me a satisfactory answer, but he didn't.

"I'll call you a little later," he said.

"Don't bother," I said, and slammed down the receiver.

Why couldn't this have happened a day later? Why did he have to hurt me on this day of all days? Though I had thought I would bawl my eyes out, I didn't feel like crying. I felt bitter. All I could think about was getting back at him for how he'd treated me.

Wasn't there a man who had the same birthday as me? Oh, and he liked me, too! I found Chen Dingleung's pager number. If he was out celebrating his birthday with friends, I could just wish him a happy birthday and then hang up—though he'd definitely think something was up if I called him from my house at ten at night to wish him a happy birthday. He'd start to get the wrong message. But revenge was all I could think about.

Chen Dingleung didn't call me back. Men are never around when women need them.

At midnight, the phone rang. I didn't know whether it was Chen Dingleung or Sam. Sam had said he'd call me later. But I didn't feel like hearing the sound of his voice, and besides, my birthday was already over. So that was how I spent my thirtieth birthday. In this apartment that he had bought me, where I was no more than his pet canary. And I'd never even realized it until now.

The phone rang again. I stood by the window, even though the man I was waiting for was nowhere to be found on the street.

The phone finally stopped ringing. There was a certain bleakness to that final ring. It couldn't have been Chen Dingleung. It had to have been Sam. If he'd rushed over before dawn to beg my forgiveness, I would've opened the door and let him in. But it was dawn, and he hadn't come. I knew then there'd be no tomorrow for us.

I hadn't expected to feel so calm and collected. I wasn't going to shed another tear for this man. I said I was going to leave him when I turned thirty, and that was what I was going to do.

I got dressed and went to work.

"Did you have a good time last night?" Jenny asked me.

"Went out for a candlelight dinner," I told her, smiling.

After work, I passed by a realtor. I went inside and asked how much I could get for my apartment. To my surprise, it had gone up by $200,000 since Sam had bought it. She asked me if I wanted to sell it, and the broker gave me her business card.

When I got home, I suddenly felt hesitant to part with my apartment, where I'd experienced so many happy memories. But was I going to spend the second half of my life hiding away in here? The answer was no.

I took a hot bath. The thirty-year-old me had turned out to be a total failure. I was just a woman who sold bras and panties for a living. What a loser!

I heard someone open the door and come in. I put on my bathrobe and stepped out to find Sam standing in my living room. He pulled me into his arms and kissed my neck.

"What about your father-in-law? Aren't you supposed to be at the hospital?" I asked him coldly.

"Why didn't you answer the phone?" he asked me.

"We're through, that's why!" I said.

"I really was at the hospital last night. If you don't believe me, there's nothing I can say," he said, looking dismayed.

"I believe that you were at the hospital last night. I know you wouldn't make that up. You're not that kind of man. If you had been trying to deceive me, I'd lose all respect for you."

Sam held me tightly, then started to loosen the belt on my bathrobe.

"No." I pried his hands away. "Last night I came to my senses. The problem isn't whether you spent my birthday with me; it's that you're someone else's husband and someone's son-in-law. That's a fact that'll never change. We've just both been slow to realize it."

Sam let go and didn't say a word. What could he say, after all? He and I both knew that there were certain realities that we couldn't change.

"You can call me after you get divorced," I said.

"Please don't be this way . . ." He pulled me towards him.

"It's the only thing I can do. You're someone's son-in-law. I should never forget that. You can't imagine what it's like to love someone who will always be part of someone else's family."

"Do you think I'm so happy?" he asked.

"I don't know. All I know is that I'm paying for my happiness with pain. Sometimes love can be a kind of suffering, and I can't handle it anymore. It's over between us."

Sam said nothing. He probably knew that this time it was for real.

"I'm going to sell this apartment, and after I sell, I'm going to give you the money."

"Do you have to sell it?" He sounded irritated.

"There's no reason why I should leave and take your money with me."

"Everything I've given you is yours to keep."

"When you bought this apartment, you thought we'd be together forever. Since that's impossible for me, I have to give it back to you. If you don't want to sell it, I'll move out."

Sam grabbed me hard and said, "Don't leave!"

I held him close. I was sure this was more painful for me than it was for him. He was the person I loved most in the world.

"You still haven't wished me a happy birthday," I told him.

He looked at me. He pressed his lips together and didn't say anything.

"You owe me a happy birthday," I insisted.

"Don't go," he said.

"Happy birthday." I prompted him.

"Happy birthday."

"Thank you," I said, smiling. "That's what I wanted to hear."

"I bought you a birthday present," he said.

"I don't want it. I don't want your gifts anymore."

"You don't even want to know what it is?"

"I don't want it to become a gift to commemorate our breakup. You already gave me a very nice gift, which is that you made me come to my senses on my thirtieth birthday. I don't want to know what it is. If I don't know, I'll wonder about it every single day. I'll wonder what it is until I'm old and gray, and even then I'll still be wondering about that year when I was thirty and what you bought for me. That way, I'll always remember you."

He let out a bitter laugh. "Are you really going to wonder every single day?"

"Uh-huh."

"You'll never guess."

"Great," I said.

I could feel his body trembling as he held me.

"Are you crying?" I stroked his face.

He wasn't crying. I'd never seen him cry before. He wasn't the type of man who'd cry. I'd overestimated him.

"You're not going to cry over me. You'll get over it soon."

"Don't sell the apartment. It's yours," he said.

"I'm sorry, but I can't not sell it. I can't live here."

"Where are you going?"

"I'll move home, or maybe rent another place."

"I'm begging you. Please don't go." He stood before me, putting aside his manly pride to plead with me. I'd never once seen him grovel like this. I'd always been his darling, his damsel in distress. Now, the way he was begging me to stay, he was the one who was like a child. It broke my heart. If you really, truly love a man, you don't ever want to see him in a state where he's groveling and helpless.

"I have no choice," I replied coldheartedly.

He just stood there, as if he'd just received the most devastating blow of his entire life. He put his hands in his pockets and forced a fleeting, pained smile.

"OK, then." He forced the words out.

He wasn't going to ask me again. He wasn't going to ask his damsel in distress, because this time she'd turned her back on him.

"I'm leaving," he said calmly. Sam had turned back into a grown man.

To my own surprise, I couldn't find the words to respond. I was a heartbeat away from telling him to stay.

At this completely inopportune moment, the phone rang.

"Good-bye." Sam opened the door.

I watched as that strong profile of his disappeared out the door.

I sprinted to pick up the phone.

"Hello? Chow Jeoi, did you call me?" It was Chen Dingleung.

"Hold on a second."

I put down the receiver and went over to the window. Sam was walking out of the building. I couldn't hold back my tears any longer.

He'd always told me that things would be perfect if we'd only met each other earlier. But no one can ever travel back in time. Funny how our meeting had been marred by bad timing, whereas our breakup seemed to have been blessed with perfect timing.

I picked up the receiver. "Hello? Sorry about that."

"No worries."

"Where are you?" I asked him.

"I'm in French Polynesia."

French Polynesia? The place that was eighteen hours behind Hong Kong?

"I came here to celebrate my fortieth birthday," Chen Dingleung said breezily.

There was no doubt about it: he and I were definitely born on the same day.

"I'm eighteen hours younger over here. I don't have to celebrate my fortieth birthday until tonight!" he said merrily.

"When you come back to Hong Kong, won't things return to normal?" I said gloomily.

"Youth is just a state of mind."

"You're only going to get an extra eighteen hours of youth."

"Eighteen hours can make a difference in a lot of things," he said.

If Sam's father-in-law had fallen ill eighteen hours later, Sam and I might not have broken up, and I might have continued to harbor the same delusions.

"What are doing with those extra eighteen hours of youth?" I was somewhat curious.

"Nothing. I'm just enjoying the time that I get to be young. That's my birthday present to myself."

"Happy birthday," I said.

"Same to you. But your birthday has actually passed, hasn't it?"

"Yes, it's over," I said.

"So why did you call me?"

"I remembered that you had the same birthday as me, so I wanted to wish you a happy birthday, that's all."

"Is that so?" He sounded disappointed.

"How did you know I was looking for you?"

"I just checked in a minute ago to see if anyone called me."

"If you're so swept up in your extra eighteen hours of youth, why did you call back?"

"I wanted to see why you'd called me."

"This long-distance call must be expensive. I'll let you go," I said.

"All right. I'll be in touch when I get back."

Why did being single lead me towards Chen Dingleung and not Sam?

"How was your birthday?" Yau Ying asked me the next day when she entered the lingerie shop.

I told her that Sam and I had broken up.

"Do you need us to keep you company while you grieve for a night—or for the next month?"

Yau Ying was truly sweet and caring. She didn't bother asking me about what had happened. She just wanted to make me feel better.

"Even a month probably won't be enough," I said. "It's going to take years. Five years of love is going to take five years to recover from."

"Don't worry, I can keep you company for five years. But do you have five years to spend being sad? You'll be thirty-five by then," Yau Ying said.

"I'm going to sell the apartment," I said.

"Why?"

"If I don't want a man, then why would I want his money?" I said.

"Lots of women run off with a man's money even if they don't want him."

"I don't hate him," I said.

After work, Yau Ying went with me to the realtor.

"Why don't you go to more than one realtor? That way, more people will come look at the apartment and you can sell it faster," Yau Ying said.

But I wasn't in any hurry to sell the apartment.

A couple of nights later, I finally got a call from Sam.

"I didn't think you'd be home," he said.

I hadn't heard his voice in three days.

"If you didn't think I'd be home, why'd you call me, then?"

"I was worried you'd pick up," he said.

I'd thought of calling him, too, and yet I knew full well that I'd try to do it when he wasn't there. Though we could hurt one another with our words, we were also comforted when we got the other's phone call.

"How have you been these past few days?" he asked me.

"I'm getting ready to sell the apartment."

"Why do you have to do that?"

"I have to give you back the money."

"I'm deeply indebted to you," he said.

"But you don't owe me money," I said.

"I don't see it that way . . ."

"I'm really selfish, aren't I?" I asked him.

"No. A woman should think about what's best for her. I'm the self-ish one. I shouldn't be wasting your time."

He didn't understand. I was more than willing to waste my time on him. I didn't mind wasting my time. But I couldn't stand the fact that he belonged to someone else's family. He didn't just belong to another woman; he belonged to a whole other family. Weren't their bonds so strong that he couldn't break them? There was no way I was going to win against a family.

"I hope you find happiness in the future," he said.

I choked back sobs.

"Jeoi, please don't fall in love with another man who's already married. Men don't have the courage to get divorced."

"You're making me cry."

"I'm sorry. I can't be there for you. You have to take care of yourself."

"I'll let you know when I get married someday." I laughed sardonically.

"Please don't . . . ," he said.

"You don't want to know?"

"I'm better off not knowing."

"You're too detached," I grumbled at him.

"If I could handle hearing the news that you got married, that'd mean that I didn't love you anymore."

"You'll stop loving me sooner or later."

"You never loved me in the first place."

"That's not true." I wiped the tears from my eyes.

"You must think I'm happy being caught in the middle."

"I don't think you're happy, but I'm positive that it's more painful for me than it is for you."

Sam said nothing.

"I have to go to bed," I said.

I couldn't fall asleep, so I went to a convenience store nearby and bought some gin and soda. When I got back, I mixed them together and gulped the drink down. It was a good makeshift sleeping pill.

***

I woke up at noon the next day after a restless night of sleep. The phone rang. I figured it was probably Sam again. It almost seemed like he didn't believe that I was really leaving him.

"I'm back!" It was Chen Dingleung.

"Oh, really?" I said groggily. I had an awful headache.

"When are you free for dinner?"

"How about tonight?" I said.

That night at dinner, Chen Dingleung scrutinized me. "Your eyes are puffy," he said.

"They are? Did you have fun during your extra eighteen hours of youth?"

"You should go there sometime."

"I'm younger than you. I don't need to go somewhere else to be young."

"Right. The place you need to go is Cherbourg."

I'd probably never go to Cherbourg. I had no interest in going by myself.

Chen Dingleung handed me a paper bag. "Happy birthday."

"Is this a birthday present?" I was taken aback.

"Why don't you open it and have a look?"

I opened the paper bag and pulled out a backless black velvet dress with a giant bow at the waist and diamond-encrusted shoulder straps. I was stunned. It was the design I'd sketched in my fashion design class—except I thought that I'd thrown it away.

"This dress looks familiar," I said.

"Of course it does. You designed it," Chen Dingleung said.

"If I sketched this design, does that mean that you secretly looked at it?"

"I didn't *secretly* look at it."

"Then how did you know?"

"You threw it in the recycling bin, which is where I got it from," he said. "I'd never made anything from someone else's design before. This was a special exception."

"How much do I owe you?"

"C'mon, it's a birthday present."

"Thank you."

"You can wear this dress when you go out to dinner with your boyfriend."

"I broke up with him," I said.

Chen Dingleung stared at me in astonishment. I detected a fleeting hint of pleasure on his face, which he quickly replaced with a more sympathetic expression.

"Did you break up on your birthday?"

"Uh-huh."

"Didn't you call to wish me a happy birthday that day?" He looked a little smug.

Chen Dingleung probably imagined that I'd been thinking of him at my darkest hour and that meant I had feelings for him. That might have been the case, but I wasn't going to admit it. A more logical explanation was that I knew he had feelings for me, and he was pretty much my only male friend. What I had really wanted at that moment was to seek out the comfort of a member of the opposite sex, which was why I thought of him.

"No, I just wanted to wish you a happy birthday." I wasn't about to give him that satisfaction.

"That's really it? You just wanted to say happy birthday?"

"Yes," I said resolutely.

"It's not because of a one in three hundred sixty-five chance of fate?" He wasn't going to let it drop.

"It's because of a one in three hundred sixty-five chance of friendship," I said. "Most couples on this planet don't have the same birthday."

"Most unhappy couples on this planet have different birthdays," Chen Dingleung said.

"Which means that there's nothing special about having the same birthday."

"If you thought of me when you and your boyfriend broke up, there's something to it," he insisted.

"There's no way I can prove to you that I don't have feelings for you, is there?" I said, suddenly angry.

"You don't have to deny it if it's true," he said arrogantly.

"You just gave me a birthday present. I didn't get you anything," I said.

"Why did you just tell me that you broke up with your boyfriend, then?" he said.

"Because I thought you were my friend. But right now, you disgust me!" I said, standing up.

Chen Dingleung looked shocked.

"I'm sorry," I said. "I shouldn't have said that. 'Disgust' is a word that's actually dear to my heart. You don't deserve my disgust. You repulse me!" I spun around and left.

I never dreamed that I'd get so upset with Chen Dingleung. Maybe I just needed someone to take my anger out on, and he just happened to irritate me right then.

"I'm sorry," Chen Dingleung said, coming up behind me and grabbing my arm.

"Let go!" I yelled and shook him off.

I ran into an elevator, but Chen Dingleung managed to hold the elevator doors open. I don't know how I found the strength, but I ruthlessly kicked him in the knee. He staggered back, and the doors closed. Inside the elevator, I couldn't help but let out a wail. I really missed Sam. Why couldn't I have the one thing I really wanted? Why did he have to be someone else's husband? What was I doing here with this Chen

Dingleung guy, feeling things out? Having lost Sam, had I also lost my last shred of dignity? When it came down to it, I missed Sam like crazy.

Even so, I couldn't run back to his side. I just couldn't. It had already been hard enough to break up with him. I couldn't go back.

I exited the elevator and stumbled onto the street.

"Chow Jeoi!" Chen Dingleung was suddenly heading towards me.

I didn't want him to see me crying. The more he kept calling out to me, the faster I ran.

"I'm sorry!" Chen Dingleung cried, catching up to me.

"I don't want to have anything to do with you!" I said.

He handed the dress to me and said, "Here. You forgot this."

I took the dress, then scrambled into a taxi.

After seeing Chen Dingleung, I loved Sam even more.

When I got home, I soaked in a hot bath. As I was getting out, someone knocked on my door. It was Kwok Seon.

"I thought you'd left for the evening. The door to the cake shop was locked when I passed by a little while ago. Come on in."

"I said I'd let you know if there was any good news," Kwok Seon said, grinning.

Although I was in no mood for good news just then, there was nothing I could do but put on a smile.

"Remember how I told you that a friend of mine invited me to an alumni association dance? Well, I met someone there."

"Who?"

"The owner of a congee shop."

"Someone who sells food, just like you!"

"That's how we hit it off. It's a very elegant restaurant in Causeway Bay. When you have some time, I'll take you there for a bowl of congee."

"Sounds good."

"Are you selling this apartment?" Kwok Seon asked. "I saw an ad for it at the realtor."

"Yes."

"So you're moving? Are you getting married?"

I shook my head.

"What's wrong?"

"Nothing."

"Has anyone come to look at the apartment?" she asked me.

"The agent has been trying to schedule appointments, but I haven't been able to make time."

"I really like this place. Why don't you sell it to me?"

"You want to buy it?"

"I've been looking for a place near the shop. Instead of selling it to someone else, why don't you sell it to me and save yourself the cost of the broker's commission?"

"Let me think about it."

Although I'd wanted to sell the apartment, I became hesitant as soon as someone said they wanted to buy it.

"Where is this?" Kwok Seon pointed at the puzzle, which I'd framed again after Sam had put it together.

"That's a restaurant in Cherbourg."

"It's gorgeous. I wish I could sell my cakes in a place like that," Kwok Seon said, admiring the puzzle.

"That restaurant might only be imaginary," I said.

For the next few days, I kept going back and forth over whether I should sell the apartment. One day, Chui Yuk and Yau Ying arrived on my doorstep with some take-out food.

"It's a shame you're selling this place," Chui Yuk said.

"The lady who owns the cake shop wants to buy it," I said.

"What is it that you have reservations about?" Yau Ying asked me.

"She can't bring herself to sell it," said Chui Yuk.

She was right. I couldn't.

"If I were you, I wouldn't sell it," Chui Yuk said. "It'll make a nice memento. It contains Sam's scent!"

It was true. I could still smell Sam's scent lingering in our bed.

"She wants to forget him. Regardless of whether you sell it or not, you do have to make a decision. If you don't sell it now, the value might go down, and you won't be able to get the price you wanted," Yau Ying said.

"I know."

"So is Chen Dingleung in the picture now?" Chui Yuk asked.

"I'm sick of that whole business," I said.

"Yu Mogwo is waiting for him to do the cover design. You should get in touch with him soon," Chui Yuk said.

"I'll call him tomorrow," I said.

"Why don't you just give him a call now?" Chui Yuk picked up the phone and handed it to me.

So I called him. When he answered, I handed the phone over to Chui Yuk and let her talk to him directly.

"Well?" I asked Chui Yuk when she had hung up.

"Why don't you want to talk to him?" Chui Yuk asked.

"What did he say?" I asked, ignoring her question.

"He wants to meet with Yu Mogwo. We made plans for lunch tomorrow. You're coming, too."

"No." I didn't want to see Chen Dingleung.

"What a beautiful dress! Where'd you get it?" Yau Ying asked. She had discovered the dress that Chen Dingleung gave me, which was lying on my bed.

"Chen Dingleung made it," I said.

"Is he madly in love with you?" Chui Yuk asked me.

Of course Chen Dingleung wasn't madly in love with me. No one had ever been madly in love with me. Even when Sam and I were together, I never felt like he was madly in love with me. Maybe there'd been a time when he was in love with me, but it hadn't ever been mad enough. If it'd been mad enough, he would've gotten divorced for me. Chen Dingleung had nothing on Sam.

I didn't go out to lunch with Chui Yuk and Yu Mogwo, but Chui Yuk came to the store afterwards to see me.

"He and Yu Mogwo really hit it off. He already has the basic concept for it. He's going to have it done in a week's time."

"He's really not going to charge you for it?"

"You really think he'd ask for money?" Chui Yuk said. "He asked about you, though."

"Oh, really? Well, since he's already agreed to design the cover for you, there's no need for me to meet with him anymore."

"He's good looking. Certainly no worse than your Sam."

"You can have him, then!"

"No thanks. He's certainly no match for Yu Mogwo!" Chui Yuk said smugly.

"I don't blame you. Every woman thinks the man she loves is the best," I said.

A week later, Chen Dingleung had finished the cover design and delivered it to Yu Mogwo. Chui Yuk showed it to me. The book was called *Attack of the Killer Bees*, and the cover featured a hand-drawn illustration of bees by Chen Dingleung. The illustration was exquisite. There was something truly menacing about it.

"Isn't he talented?" Chui Yuk said. "This is an important book for Yu Mogwo. If it's a hit, he won't have to worry anymore about no one wanting to publish his work."

"It's going to be a hit," I said.

"Thank you." Chui Yuk seemed touched. "So have you decided whether you're going to sell your place or not?" It was a question I had to face. When a woman leaves a man, she's forced to come to a decision on many things. But I didn't have an answer for her.

Later that day, I went to the cake shop to see Kwok Seon. She was getting ready to lock up.

"Do you still want to buy my apartment?" I asked her.

"I really do fancy it. But if you don't want to sell it, I don't want to pressure you. I bought a house once before. It was the place where my husband and I lived for more than twenty years. We couldn't bear to sell it. Along the outside walls of that house, there were all these spots that were infested with termites. The night before we moved out, I suddenly started trying to hunt down their nest, and I remember watching them crawling everywhere. I was absolutely fed up with them. But when I left, I realized I was sad to leave them. I completely understand how it feels to give up a home that you love," Kwok Seon told me tenderly.

"Tell me about it. Termites and your love for someone can be very similar. They both have the power to totally ruin things." I laughed bitterly.

I asked Daihoi to handle the transaction, and he agreed to do it for me pro bono. I took him and Yau Ying out to dinner to thank them.

"Have you found a place for yourself yet?" Yau Ying asked me.

"Not yet," I said. "The rents are too high in this neighborhood, and the spaces are too big."

"I know of some buildings in Central with smaller units, and the rent's not too bad. They should be fine for one person," Daihoi said.

So Daihoi found an apartment for me. The building was located near the city center, right next to an escalator. The unit I looked at had a window that actually faced the escalator. There was only a twelve- to fifteen-foot gap in between. If you stood at the window, you could see the passersby and hear the escalator's motor.

"It's going to be noisy!" said Yau Ying, who had accompanied me.

"That's why the rent is so low," the landlady said.

"I'll take it," I said.

"Won't the noise bother you?" Yau Ying asked me.

"It'll be fine if I just keep the window shut, don't you think?"

After the landlady and I had taken care of the paperwork, Yau Ying and I went to eat at a fast-food restaurant nearby.

"I honestly never thought you'd consider a building like that," Yau Ying said.

"But the rent is so cheap! If I'm going to be self-reliant, I have to be frugal," I said.

"The problem with you is that you're too conscientious for your own good. You really don't have to sell the apartment."

"I don't want to get any kind of help from Sam," I said.

"Do you want me and Daihoi to help you move?"

"I haven't even thought about the move yet."

"The law firm has a car for clients that you can borrow."

"Thank you," I said.

"Oh please—you don't have to thank me! When you don't have love, you need friends. If I were the one going through heartbreak, I'd be moving in with you! That's why I'm here to help."

"Are things all right with you and Daihoi?"

"If there's been no progress, does that mean that we're regressing?"

"I don't think that's how emotions work," I said.

"Daihoi's been falling asleep during sex again. Plus we're doing it less and less often. Lately it's been like neither of us is even interested."

"This is in spite of the fact that you've been wearing sexy lingerie?"

Yau Ying laughed cruelly. "Sexy lingerie is only there to titillate. Once the novelty wears off, it's useless."

I recalled when Sam and I made love for the last time. Both of us were happy then. "If you have good sex right before you break up, it'll be your fondest memory," I said.

"It's so true! It's a lot better than breaking up and not being able to remember the last time you did it."

"I can remember quite a few of the times when Sam and I made love," I recalled.

"Really? How many times?" Yau Ying asked me, grinning.

"A lot!" I said, blushing.

"I have a few of those memories, too. But when I think about it now, I feel so hopeless. Those times when Daihoi and I were the happiest seem like such a long time ago."

"I once asked Sam if he ever got tired of always making love to the same woman."

"What did he say?'

"He said no."

"I used to think that women didn't have their own sexual needs—that was in my twenties—and that making love was something you did to satisfy a man. But ever since I turned thirty, I've realized that I have needs, too."

"I wonder if when a man reminisces about a woman, he thinks about the first time they ever made love."

"I don't know."

"Men are always so eager to move from one experience to the next. I wonder if they even think about which time was the best," I said.

"I'll have to find a man so I can ask him," Yau Ying said, covering her mouth as she laughed.

When I got home that night, I went over to the bed and pressed my body into the sheets. The last time Sam and I made love was a memory I truly cherished. It was too bad that the new place was so small. It meant I couldn't take the bed with me.

The night before I was supposed to move, I packed up all my belongings. I couldn't take most of the furniture. Since I couldn't take the bed, I took the sheets Chui Yuk had given me and the comforter Sam had bought me. I removed the framed puzzle of the Cherbourg restaurant from the wall and wrapped it in newspaper.

Someone knocked at the door. It was Kwok Seon.

"Is there anything I can do to help?" she asked, looking around. "I really like the way this place is decorated. I don't think I'll change a thing. Do you have a new phone number yet?"

"I just signed up, so I still don't have one yet."

"I've heard that these days you can keep your old phone number after you move."

"I need a fresh start," I said. "Any news on the congee shop owner?"

"We're going out for vegetarian food on Lantau Island tomorrow night. Only old people would call that a date. But we hope to take ballroom dancing lessons together in the future."

"Is he going to move in with you?"

"Why? This is my own little corner of the universe."

"Have the two of you done the deed yet?"

"People become more reserved as they grow older. Plus I don't dare. The last man who saw me naked took off running," Kwok Seon told me.

"Took off running?"

"Maybe it's because I take care of my appearance that he misjudged me and assumed that I've maintained my figure equally well," Kwok Seon said with a chuckle.

"Did he really take off running?" In my mind, the scene was just too comical.

"No. He just made his pager beep. Then he said someone was looking for him and left in a hurry."

"That's so awful!"

"He probably imagined that I had these firm, perky breasts. When he saw what they were really like, he was terrified."

"They're not as bad as you say they are," I said.

"It's kind of funny looking back on it."

"If this congee shop owner runs away, he's dead meat!" I told her.

"That's right! I'll butcher him and use him to make congee." Kwok Seon paused. "Did you and Mr. Tong have a fight?"

"It's not as simple as that." At the mention of his name, I was overwhelmed with sadness.

"He seems like such a nice man, and you love each other so much. I expected you two to get married."

You can't really trust the observations of a woman who makes men take off running. In any case, Kwok Seon had guessed wrong. Seeing that I didn't want to talk about it, she didn't press me on the subject.

"You're even leaving me the sofa, the bed, and the fridge. I don't have to buy a thing. This refrigerator looks like it's brand new!" Kwok Seon swung open the door to the fridge.

"What? You still haven't eaten your birthday cake?" Kwok Seon discovered the rose-shaped birthday cake that Sam had ordered for me. It was rock hard.

On Sunday morning, Yau Ying, Daihoi, Chui Yuk, and Yu Mogwo came to help me move.

I had carefully inspected every last nook to make sure that I didn't leave anything behind. As I looked at the bed, I felt sad that I'd never be able to crawl into it again. Why was I suddenly unwilling to part with the apartment that Sam had given me? Was it because I was naive and full of pride? This bed had once been a token of his love. Soon, all I would have left of him was the scorpion hanging around my neck. I slumped onto the bed and cried.

"I knew you'd do this," Chui Yuk said, sitting down beside me.

I brushed away my tears.

Yau Ying, who was standing at the doorway, said, "You already sold that bed to someone else. It's time to go."

She was always the rational one.

"I knew all along that you wouldn't be able to go through with this. You shouldn't have broken up with him."

I got off the bed and stood up. "Let's go!" Then I stopped. "Hold on." I went into the kitchen and opened the fridge. I took out the birthday cake that Sam had given me.

"Did you buy a cake? I'm ravenous," Chui Yuk said.

"It's gone bad," I said.

The bed in my new apartment was built into a recess in the wall. The craftsmanship was shoddy, and there was a crack between the wall and the bed. I made the bed with the sheets from Chui Yuk and the comforter from Sam, but the bed was too small, and the linens were too big.

"What about your phone?" Yau Ying asked me.

"Someone's coming over tomorrow to install it."

"I don't have my cell phone on me," Yau Ying said.

"Don't worry about it," I said.

"Daihoi, can you lend your cell phone to Chow Jeoi?"

"I'll get by without a phone for a day," I said. I really didn't want to take Daihoi's cell phone. Plus he didn't look enthusiastic.

"What's the big deal?" Yau Ying said picking up Daihoi's cell phone from the desk. "You just moved in. You don't know the area or the neighbors. What are you going to do if you need something?" So I took the phone.

My friends eventually had to leave, and there I was, all alone. The silence was truly terrifying. At noon, Daihoi's cell phone rang.

"Hello?" I answered.

"Hello. May I speak to Daihoi?" a woman with a pleasant-sounding voice asked me.

"He's not here," I said.

"Isn't this his cell phone?"

"It is, but he's not here."

"Oh." The woman sounded disappointed.

"Who's calling?" I asked.

"I'm a friend of his," the woman answered briskly.

"Would you like me to tell him that you called?" I asked.

"No thanks." The woman hung up.

This woman's voice sounded so sweet. It sounded familiar. Who could she be? What was her relationship to Daihoi? Did Yau Ying know about her? Was she Daihoi's secret mistress?

I took out the framed puzzle and placed it in front of the window in the bedroom. The restaurant and skies over Cherbourg were a vast improvement over the escalator.

Daihoi's phone rang again early the next morning.

"Hello?" I answered it.

The caller hung up. Was it that woman again?

Around noon, I went to give Daihoi his phone back. Yau Ying had stepped out for lunch.

"Did you sleep OK in your new place?" he asked.

"It wasn't so bad."

"Did anyone call for me?"

"There was a woman," I said.

"Oh." Daihoi looked a little embarrassed. "Did she say who she was?"

I shook my head.

"It might've been a client. There's one annoying client who's been calling me almost every day." I got the feeling that he wasn't entirely telling the truth. Just then, Yau Ying walked in.

"Chow Jeoi, what are you doing here? There's no hurry to give the phone back."

"My phone was installed this morning. Here's my new number." I handed her a slip of paper with the number on it.

Yau Ying winked at me, signaling for me to look at the woman who'd just walked in. She was young, probably around twenty-four years old, and she wore a white silk blouse with a midlength skirt. She was very busty, and I realized it had to be Olivia Wu, the 36C that Yau Ying had been talking about. She was busy talking to a secretary.

"I'll walk you out." Yau Ying clearly didn't want to talk to me about Olivia in front of Daihoi.

When we got outside, she grabbed my hand and said, "Totally over the top, isn't it?"

"Even bigger than Chui Yuk."

"She especially likes getting up close to Daihoi. It's so disgusting!" I'd heard Olivia speak, and she didn't sound like the woman who'd called Daihoi last night.

"Where are you off to?" Yau Ying asked.

I opened my purse and showed Yau Ying the check I'd written.

"I'm giving this to Sam," I said.

"God, $2.8 million! What a shame!" Yau Ying was even less willing to part with the money than I was.

"Sometimes money is just a number," I said.

Because really, if you couldn't be with the person you loved, what good was money?

"You're planning to hand it to him in person?" Yau Ying asked.

"I'm going to put it in the mail." I didn't have the courage to meet Sam face-to-face.

"You're going to mail a check for $2.8 million? Isn't that awfully risky?"

"It's not like it's cash."

"Wouldn't it be safer to have someone deliver it? Do you want our company's courier to do it? Sam's office is nearby."

"But . . ." I was hesitant.

Yau Ying went to the reception desk and brought back an envelope.

"Where's the check?"

I handed it over. Yau Ying folded the check inside a sheet of white paper and slipped it inside the envelope.

"Write the address on the outside." Yau Ying handed me a pen.

I wrote the address of Sam's company on the outside.

A messenger stepped into the office just then. Yau Ying handed him the envelope and said, "Please deliver it to this address. And get signature confirmation."

The messenger readily accepted the envelope and got onto the elevator.

"It's much safer this way," Yau Ying said.

I was instantly filled with regret.

"I want my check back!" I burst into tears.

I looked at the bank of elevators. One elevator had stopped at the top floor. Another elevator was going down. I ran down the stairs.

As I exited the building, I discovered that the messenger was already far off in the distance.

"Wait up!" I called.

People on the street turned and stared at me. The only person who didn't turn around was the messenger. I finally caught up to him and latched onto his backpack, right there in the middle of the street.

"What are you doing?" he asked me.

"Give me back my envelope."

"Which envelope is yours?"

I grabbed the envelope for Sam out of the backpack.

"This one," I said.

Yau Ying caught up to us.

I clutched the envelope. I'd just come to my senses. I wasn't ready to part with it.

"What on earth are you doing? You just ran down from the fifteenth floor all the way to the street. I'm so out of breath, I'm dying!

You really can't bring yourself to give that money to Sam, can you?" Yau Ying was panting as she spoke.

"This isn't about the money. I can't accept the fact that I've seen Sam for the last time. I have to give this check to him in person."

I put the envelope in my purse. Holding my purse tightly against my chest, I headed to work. I waited until closing time, when Anna and Jenny had left, before I finally gathered the courage to call Sam. He sounded happy to hear my voice and we made plans to meet at our favorite French restaurant.

Sam showed up right on time.

"Did you move yet?" he asked me when he sat down. "Where are you moving to?"

I handed him the check. "This is for you."

"I said I didn't want it." He pushed it back towards me.

"Did you ever love me?" I asked.

"You still have to ask?" Sam smiled sadly.

"Well, I'm asking you to accept this check."

"I'm telling you, don't make me do it."

"If you loved me, then you should accept this check." I put the check inside his bag.

"Do you have to do this?"

I nodded stubbornly.

"When are you having a child?" I asked him, smiling.

"A child?"

"A child with your wife. Like a real family," I said grimly.

"You think that as soon as you leave, I'm going to instantly go home and have a child? You've never understood me."

"So you're saying that you've never wanted children?"

Sam stared at me, speechless.

As I leaned over to take a sip of my soup, the scorpion charm on my necklace suddenly came loose and tumbled into the bowl, splattering soup onto my clothes and face. Sam quickly retrieved the scorpion charm.

"It's really hot!" I said.

Sam took out his handkerchief and wiped my face.

"I'm going to go wash my face. And I'm going to clean this off while I'm at it," I said, grabbing the scorpion charm back.

Once inside the restroom, I started to cry. I wouldn't let myself cry in front of him. Why was it that when it came time to say good-bye, I felt so reluctant for things to end? I deeply resented the fact that he wouldn't get a divorce. I rinsed off the scorpion charm under the faucet, then dried it with a towel. The clasp had come loose, causing the charm to slip off. I never should have worn the necklace in the first place. I dried my eyes and went back.

"Is something wrong?" Sam asked me.

I shook my head. But could I really hide it from him? Though I had the eyes of a person who'd been crying, there was no real proof.

"There are still stains on your blouse," Sam said.

"Who cares? Who doesn't have any stains on their clothes? These stains will give me something to remember this meal by."

"Have you really made up your mind?"

"Why? Do you want me to wait for you? You've never, ever asked me before to wait for you. If you'd asked me to wait, there'd still be hope for us. But you never did even that much."

"I just want you to be happy after you leave me," he said, crestfallen.

"You don't have to be so nice to me. Why don't you go home and be a good husband?"

We finished the meal in silence. I'd been too idealistic. I had thought that two people who once loved each other could break up over a candlelight dinner. But because we'd once loved each other, there was no way we could be our old selves again. All we could do was hurt each other one last time.

"I'll take you home," he said.

"You don't have to."

"Are you scared of me knowing where you live?"

"How about if I take you home instead?" I asked him. "I've never done that before. I've never even seen your building. I don't even know what floor you live on. Now you can relax and let me take you home. Don't worry—I won't do anything crazy like come knocking on your door."

Sam looked hesitant.

"What? You don't think it's a good idea?"

Even now, he still didn't trust me. He thought I was the kind of woman who'd come knocking on his door and cause trouble.

"Are you afraid I'll stalk you?"

"I'd never thought about it before. She knows that you exist. I don't want you to get hurt, that's all. You think I'm more selfish than I really am."

"Is that a yes?" I said.

"All right," he finally answered.

It was the first time I'd ever been to his place. Deep down, I was actually a little scared.

"I live in 12A," he said.

"I'll take you upstairs," I said boldly.

"OK." He seemed to understand that there was no stopping me.

When we reached the twelfth floor, my heart was pounding. I didn't dare to look over at him.

"This is where I live," he said.

My heart felt as if it were being ripped apart. Never in my dreams had I imagined that I'd find myself standing before his home, the home that he and another woman shared. What would I do if that woman suddenly walked out of their apartment, or if she came home just then?

"I'll stop here," I said timidly, stepping back into the elevator. "Thanks for letting me take you home . . ."

I hadn't finished what I was going to say when Sam followed me and pulled me out of the elevator.

"Don't go," he said, holding me in his arms.

"I'm not allowed to go? What, are you going to invite me in?" Sam took my face in his hands and kissed me—right then and there, outside the door to his apartment, where that woman was close at hand. That kiss we shared was simultaneously crazy and thrilling. Sam must have gone completely mad.

I deeply cherish the memory of that kiss. I won't deny it.

But when all was said and done, it was over between us, and he had to go home.

"Even if you walk a thousand miles to take a friend home, you still have to part ways. That's how the saying goes, right?" I asked him.

Sam was silent.

"I have to go," I said.

"You never told me where you live."

"It doesn't matter."

"I still have your birthday present."

"Didn't I say that I didn't want to know what it was? Go inside! I don't want to see a woman come out of there."

I pressed the button to call the elevator.

The elevator arrived.

"Good-bye," I told him.

Sam stood there dejectedly. This was probably the first time he'd ever lost to a woman.

As the elevator doors closed, I caught one last glimpse of him through the crack. I'd never be the woman who went home with him.

As I sat inside a taxi, I peered up at the twelfth floor. The lights were on in one unit, but I didn't know if it was Sam's. I wondered if he'd wiped the traces of my lipstick from his lips before he walked through the door.

5

Do You Still Love Me?

The following week, I discovered that Sam hadn't cashed the check. The money was still in my account. I'd known all along that he didn't want it. I'd wanted to give the money back to him, but then I thought: If he really did take the money back, would I be disappointed? I went so far as to doubt whether he'd ever loved me.

Chui Yuk said, "If he actually cashes the check, you'll never be able to look back fondly on your relationship."

An entire month passed, and the money remained intact in my bank account. I hadn't been mistaken. Sam was a good person. But I wouldn't ever have the good fortune of being his wife. Maybe someday, six months from now, a year from now, even ten years from now, he'd wake up and go cash the check.

Then, one day Chui Yuk said, "Yu Mogwo wants to invite you ladies to dinner with us this Thursday night. What do you say?"

"As long as we don't talk about book sales figures." I was baffled at how Yu Mogwo could be so upbeat this time around.

"He's been really optimistic ever since he got back from the States. If things stayed the way they were before, then I'd be worried!" Chui Yuk told me.

"I'm thinking of starting a publishing house," Yu Mogwo announced when he sat down.

We were at an Italian restaurant with an outdoor patio in Sai Kung Town.

"You've never mentioned this before." Chui Yuk, her hand on her chin, listened attentively to what he was saying.

"Hong Kong is a tough place to set up a publishing firm," Chen Dingleung said. I'd thawed out enough in the past few weeks to agree to see him again.

"A friend of mine and I are going to form a partnership," Yu Mogwo said. "In addition to publishing my own science-fiction novels, we're going to travel to Japan and buy the foreign rights for manga, then translate and publish it here in Hong Kong. This friend of mine knows a lot about Japan. If we can get the rights to manga that's going to be well received here, we can make a lot of money." Yu Mogwo seemed pleased.

"Sounds like a great idea!" Chui Yuk was gazing at Yu Mogwo with admiration.

The next day, Chui Yuk came to see me. As it turned out, Yu Mogwo had no start-up capital.

"How much does he need?" I asked Chui Yuk.

"He and his partner need to come up with $300,000."

"That much?"

"They need money to go to Japan and then buy the rights for a whole bunch of manga. You can't just buy them for one title. That's the biggest expense. They also have to rent an office and hire two or three employees to do printing, typesetting, marketing, and so on. All those things require money. Every book will cost tens of thousands of dollars to produce," she explained.

"So if he doesn't have any money, how's he going to start a publishing firm?" I asked Chui Yuk.

"It's so like him not to think about money. He's just so impulsive—he never thinks through the practicalities."

Chui Yuk didn't seem to mind Yu Mogwo's way of doing things. This man, who had no real knowledge of his own capabilities, was simply going to charge forwards and leave all the problems to a woman to fix. Wasn't that rather irresponsible?

"He thinks I still have savings," Chui Yuk said.

"You already gave him your entire savings when he went to the States. He still thinks you have money?" I said, growing angry.

"He didn't know that was my entire savings. It's all because I don't live frugally, and I buy bras that cost hundreds of dollars."

"I can't touch the money in my bank account. Sam could withdraw it at any moment." I knew Chui Yuk wanted my help.

"I know that."

"I have $54,000 in my account, but that's it. It's my entire savings, but I can lend it to you."

"It won't be nearly enough." Chui Yuk sighed.

"Talk to Yau Ying," I said.

"I really don't want to borrow from friends. That'd be going overboard. He should just borrow from a commercial lender. I've heard that if your salary is $10,000, they'll let you borrow $20,000."

"If you go to a commercial lender, won't the interest be high? Plus you don't have a stable income. They might not approve you for a loan."

Chui Yuk left disappointed. She didn't get in touch for a few days.

***

"There's a way I can get $300,000," Chui Yuk told me the next time I saw her.

"How?"

"Someone approached me about being in a video."

"You can make that much money by being in a video?"

"Well, of course most don't pay that well."

"You're not talking about a porn flick, are you?"

"I don't have to get completely naked. I just need to act bolder and sexier."

"You're not going to do it, are you?"

"They're going to give me $300,000."

"You're not even famous, and they're going to give you $300,000? Do you have to get naked?"

"I have to show my breasts," Chui Yuk said finally.

"It's a porn flick, isn't it? Don't do it."

"No."

"Are you doing this for Yu Mogwo? If he doesn't get the money, he can't start a publishing house. It's not like he's going to die."

"This is his dream. He's already started looking for an office space."

"Does he know that you're going to be in this video?"

"He can't find out."

"If he finds out, he's going to break up with you."

"He's not going to find out. He's totally illiterate when it comes to technology."

"What if one of his friends sees it?"

"He doesn't have that many friends. They're not into that sort of thing, either."

"What if he just happens to see it?"

"He might not know it's me. I'm going to get a perm and put on a ton of makeup. Worst case, I'll say they told me they were going to replace my face with a famous celebrity's."

"Don't do it, Chui Yuk! I have $54,000 here—take it!" I handed her the check.

"Save it for yourself!" Chui Yuk laughed triumphantly. "I know the producer, who knows I need the money and is giving me $300,000! The normal rate is $200,000."

"Did you already agree to do it?" I was in utter disbelief.

"I'm going to sign the contract tomorrow."

"Are you sure about this?"

"Didn't I say that I'd do anything for Yu Mogwo?" Chui Yuk said, smiling.

"I can ask Sam for help. I can borrow $300,000 from him," I told Chui Yuk.

Chui Yuk took my hand. "You're such a decent person. You really are my best friend in the entire world. But if you ask Sam if you can borrow money from him, surely it'll make things worse for you. If a woman breaks up with a man, then goes and asks him for money, he'll despise her. It'll ruin all of the wonderful memories that the two of you share. That's a much bigger sacrifice than for me to show my breasts."

"But you're a woman. What are you supposed to do after this?"

"I can't express how happy I am to be a woman. How else would I ever be able to make money off these two little things on my chest? Please don't make this out to be worse than it actually is. A well-known Japanese photographer is going to be shooting it. He's done a lot of photo books for female celebrities. This video is going to be totally artistic. It's going to be sexy, not pornographic. I don't have to have sex with any male lead. You have to take advantage of being young and get some beautiful pictures taken of yourself!"

"But this video is going to be sold to the public. Any man could just buy one and watch it."

"They can already look at me on the street. Besides, they won't even know who I am. Wouldn't you agree that I have a great figure?"

"They wouldn't have asked you if you didn't."

"So wouldn't it be a complete waste if I didn't do it?"

"They're telling you all these things to flatter you, aren't they?"

"Listen to me. When a woman has a great figure, a day will come when it's a thing of the past. The only thing in life that I have to be proud of—aside from Yu Mogwo—is my figure. A few years from now, after I've had Yu Mogwo's babies, am I still going to have my figure? What's wrong with keeping a memento?"

"Let me ask you a question. If Yu Mogwo didn't need $300,000, would you still be doing this?"

"No, I wouldn't."

"So there you go. This idea that you should get some beautiful pictures of yourself is bullshit. You're deluded."

"Well, I'm doing it. So why not hope for the best?"

I felt sad. I wanted to tell Yu Mogwo.

When I met up with Yau Ying for coffee later that evening, I told her about Chui Yuk's plans.

"If you tell Yu Mogwo, Chui Yuk's going to be mad at you," Yau Ying said.

"If she goes through with it, she's going to regret it."

"Why are you trying to stop her from making a sacrifice for her man?"

I'd expected Yau Ying to take my side. I never would've guessed she'd be more open minded than I was.

"For a man like that, would you call it a sacrifice? It doesn't seem like he's even financially independent." Yu Mogwo was starting to disgust me.

Yau Ying sighed. "Women always think their own man is worth making sacrifices for. It's other women who don't think those men are worth those women's sacrifices."

"But of course!" I cackled.

"Daihoi seems to have gotten involved with another woman," Yau Ying told me, sounding agonized.

"How'd you find out?"

"It's just a sense I get. I don't have any proof."

I remembered the woman who called Daihoi on his cell phone.

"The first day that I moved into my new apartment, remember how you lent me Daihoi's cell phone? A woman called for him that night."

"Why didn't you tell me sooner?" Yau Ying said, growing tense.

"She didn't say anything. I thought she and Daihoi might just be friends or that she might be one of his clients."

"It could be her. What did she sound like?"

"Very pleasant. I felt like I'd heard her voice somewhere before."

"Where?"

"I can't remember."

"Is it Olivia Wu?"

"No way. You think it's her?"

"I did before. But I no longer think so. Daihoi wouldn't go for her type."

"You shouldn't be suspicious of Daihoi. Men don't like it when women are suspicious of them."

"That's why he doesn't know I'm suspicious of him."

"That's right! You're terrible!" I suddenly recalled what Daihoi had told me when I went out to lunch with him.

"Not only does he feel like you don't distrust him, he also thinks that you don't even care about him!"

Yau Ying let out a self-deprecating laugh. "If only I were more like Chui Yuk."

"Like her?"

"Loving without so much as a second thought."

"Yeah, she's really sweet."

I didn't know whether it was actually a problem between Chui Yuk and Yu Mogwo, but Chui Yuk was too giving. If Yu Mogwo ever ceased to be faithful, it'd be a huge blow to Chui Yuk. But in Yau Ying and Daihoi's case, it was more complicated.

"Every relationship comes with its own trials and tribulations," I said.

"You probably had it the best out of the three of us, with Sam," Yau Ying said.

"What do you mean?"

"You two broke up right when you loved each other the most. That's the best way to do it."

"I don't think so at all," I said.

"I didn't think anyone could do that, but you did."

"I've regretted breaking up with him every time. I always felt so bad afterwards that I kept getting back together with him. Our breakup is for the best."

Yau Ying and I took the minibus back to the store. The driver had the radio on, and the host of the program had a lovely voice.

"It's her voice!" I said grabbing Yau Ying's sleeve.

"That's her?" Yau Ying seemed confounded. It was as if the suspect was suddenly in our midst.

"I've heard this voice before. It's so alluring," I said.

"Are you sure it's her?"

Of course I couldn't be sure—I'd only heard her voice once on the phone—but it was a striking one.

"They sound really similar, but I can't say for certain."

"Excuse me, driver, what station are we listening to?" Yau Ying asked the driver.

"How am I supposed to know? Whatever station gets a clear signal," the driver said.

Yau Ying went up to the front of the bus to see for herself, then she looked at her watch. "Right now it's five past ten, so it's the evening show."

"Even if she is the woman who called Daihoi, it doesn't mean that there's anything suspicious about their relationship," I said.

"I have to investigate. I have to find out what this woman looks like. Are you free around this time tomorrow?"

The next day, Yau Ying came looking for me.

"Last night I got home at ten forty," she said. "Daihoi was listening to that woman's radio show."

"It could've been a coincidence."

"Let's go to the station tonight," Yau Ying said.

"What do you actually want to do there?"

Yau Ying wanted to stand outside the station and wait for her to come out.

That night, we met up outside the station.

"We're like rock-star groupies, hanging out like this," I said.

Yau Ying led me over to the bushes by the side, and said, "If we stand here, we don't have to worry about people seeing us. Also, Daihoi won't discover us if he comes to pick her up when she finishes work."

"If you really do see Daihoi coming to pick her up when she finishes work, what are you going to do?"

"I don't know."

"If I were you, I wouldn't go up to her."

"Why not?"

"I'd be afraid of seeing the man I love in love with another woman," I said.

"That must be her!" Yau Ying said.

A tall woman with short hair came out of the radio station. She was wearing jeans and a black halter top under a leather jacket.

"Whoa! 34C!" I sized up her measurements in the blink of an eye. Her figure was rather average, but her breasts were the most beautiful kind of all—the kind that are like a pair of mangoes.

"34C." Yau Ying appeared to have suffered a crushing blow.

"We don't know for certain that it's her," I said.

"Go ask," Yau Ying prodded me.

The woman stood on the sidewalk, waiting for a taxi. Summoning my courage, I stepped up and said, "I'm a loyal fan. I just love listening to your show."

The woman appeared slightly stunned at first, but then she smiled. She'd probably never seen anyone as old as me loitering outside the station doors like a crazed young fan waiting for her idol.

"Thank you. What are you doing here so late?"

I recognized the sound of her voice. She was the one.

A taxi pulled up right in front of us.

"Bye!" She called as she climbed into the taxi.

My pager went off. It was Chui Yuk.

"Well? Was it her?" Yau Ying asked as she came over from the other side of the street.

I nodded.

Yau Ying hailed a cab.

"Where are we going?" I asked her.

"We're following her." Yau Ying dragged me into the car.

I used Yau Ying's cell phone to call Chui Yuk.

"Chow Jeoi, where are you?"

"I'm in a cab with Yau Ying."

"I want to see you. I'll come meet you guys," Chui Yuk said.

"Don't hang up yet," I told Chui Yuk.

The taxi we were following eventually stopped in front of a convenience store on Lock Road.

"I'm at a convenience store on Lock Road," I told Chui Yuk, then hung up.

The woman went into the convenience store, paid for a bowl of noodles and a beer, then started eating inside. Yau Ying and I stood outside watching her.

Suddenly someone came up from behind us, scaring us half to death. It was Chui Yuk.

"How'd you get here so fast?" I was amazed.

"I happened to be in the area," Chui Yuk said. "What are you guys doing here?"

"Shh!" I gestured for her to stop talking.

When the woman had finished her noodles, she left the shop and entered a nearby apartment building.

"Who is she?" Chui Yuk asked.

"Daihoi didn't show up," I told Yau Ying.

"Will you two come grab a drink with me, please?" Chui Yuk asked, with a pleading note in her voice. "Today was the first day of production!"

It was only then that I noticed how much makeup she was wearing and that her hair had been permed into an unruly mess of curls. She was wearing a tank top and a miniskirt with a jacket draped over her shoulders.

Chui Yuk covered her face and started to cry. "The work is really hard!"

"Let's find somewhere to get a drink," Yau Ying said, putting her arm around Chui Yuk.

We went to a nearby bar and grabbed a table. I felt bad that I hadn't been looking after Chui Yuk. I had no idea that she'd already started filming.

"Why are you upset?" Yau Ying asked Chui Yuk.

"Did the director try to take advantage of you or make you do something you didn't want to do?" I asked. Chui Yuk dried her eyes and looked at Yau Ying and me. Then suddenly, as though seized with anguish, she threw her head into her arms on the table and started bawling.

"Tell us what happened," Yau Ying said.

"Do you know what it feels like to strip naked in front of other people? All these men I don't even know!" Chui Yuk continued sobbing.

"I told you not to do it."

"I'll get used to it soon," Chui Yuk said, wiping her eyes.

"Do you think the price you paid today was worth it? Won't you regret this in the future?" I asked her indignantly.

"I've never loved a man this much in my life," Chui Yuk said through gritted teeth. "His happiness is my happiness."

"Does he know you're crying right now?" I asked.

"Why does he need to know that I'm crying? His publishing house is holding its launch tomorrow. Yu Mogwo is at the new office right now, getting everything ready. He finally has a business of his own. Why should I make him watch me cry?"

I was at a loss for words. I'd thought that I was self-sacrificing, but Chui Yuk was even more self-sacrificing. I could never do what she had just done. Or maybe it wasn't that I couldn't do it—it was that I'd never been given an opportunity to make that kind of sacrifice for someone I loved.

"Why were you guys following that woman just now?" Chui Yuk asked us.

I told Chui Yuk the whole story behind the woman.

"But you still don't have any proof that she's the other woman!" Chui Yuk took Yau Ying's hand and tried to comfort her.

"She's a 34C, isn't that right?" Yau Ying asked me.

"According to my expert judgment, that's about her measurement," I said. "Daihoi wouldn't fall in love with a 34C, would he?"

"Well, 34C isn't that big," Chui Yuk said.

"You're prettier than that woman," I told Yau Ying.

"You think?" All of Yau Ying's self-confidence seemed to have vanished.

"If you don't believe me, ask Chui Yuk."

Chui Yuk nodded and said, "I've always thought that you were really pretty."

"Thanks, you two." Yau Ying forced a smile.

"Hasn't Daihoi ever complimented you?" Chui Yuk asked her.

"No matter how beautiful a woman is, that beauty becomes ordinary in a man's eyes after a while," she said.

"Are you guys going to interrogate Daihoi?" Chui Yuk asked.

"No," I said. "Yau Ying has never even told him that she loves him. How's she ever going to interrogate him?"

"If Yu Mogwo ever had another woman, he'd be dead meat," Chui Yuk said, gnashing her teeth.

"You're someone who's afraid to lose," I said to Yau Ying.

"Who's not?" Yau Ying shot the question back at me.

"You're so afraid that you won't even allow for an opportunity in which you could lose," I said.

"If she and Daihoi really are involved, what are you going to do?" Chui Yuk asked.

"Let's get out of here!" Yau Ying stood up and left the bar.

Outside, the sky was cold and desolate. Chui Yuk had lost her honor for $300,000, Yau Ying might have lost Daihoi, and I'd already lost Sam. Why had we each lost so much?

Back at my apartment later that night, I tossed and turned in my bed. Yau Ying hadn't changed much since she was a kid. She was still too strong.

Sometimes I felt that being too strong was also a kind of weakness. I removed the picture of Cherbourg from my window. The escalator had been shut off for the day, and a few people were slowly making their way up the stairs. I'd often imagined that one day I'd see a familiar pair of legs, and they would be Sam's. He would be passing by my window, and I'd reach out and grab him by the leg. But he didn't come around this neighborhood very often. I flipped around the puzzle so that it faced out the window. If one day Sam happened to walk down this street and notice the puzzle in the window, he'd know that I was inside, and maybe he'd knock.

The next day, Yau Ying called.

"Are you going to the station tonight to wait for that woman again?" I asked her.

"You used to be the other woman. Sam's wife must've felt the way I do now, right?"

"I never once thought about how she felt," I said.

"She must've despised you. The other woman is always so despicable."

I felt slightly ashamed, like Yau Ying was attacking me.

"You should try being the other woman. The other woman isn't always despicable. It's fate that's despicable," I said.

"So, are you going to the station tonight?" I asked her again.

"Of course!" she said.

Yau Ying had called the station and discovered that the woman's name was Tou Lei.

Yau Ying and I arrived outside the station at 10:50. Tou Lei left the station at 11:05. She got into a cab, just as she had the night before. She got out at the same convenience store, had something to eat there, then walked home.

"It might not be her after all," I said.

The following night, Yau Ying drove Daihoi's convertible to pick me up.

"We're driving to the station?" I asked her.

"Get in!" she said. "I want to know the facts. Now."

At 10:30, Yau Ying parked the car in front of the station. It was pouring.

"There's no way Daihoi is going to show up here tonight. The weather's terrible. Besides, he's never shown up here before," I said.

I truly regretted identifying Tou Lei's voice. If there really was something going on between Daihoi and Tou Lei, things would be over between him and Yau Ying.

At 10:50, Yau Ying said, "Get in the back." I climbed from the front passenger seat into the backseat.

"Can you get down low?" she asked.

I crouched down in the backseat.

We listened to Tou Lei's radio show while we were waiting for her to come out. That evening, she played a lot of love songs. The last song she played was, much to my surprise, "I Will Wait for You." I didn't dare listen to that song anymore, and I hadn't expected to hear it. Was Tou Lei waiting for someone, too? Whether out of reason or emotion, I should've been sympathetic towards Yau Ying. But I didn't want Tou Lei to get caught. I silently prayed that she wouldn't come out the door.

After the last song ended, Yau Ying pulled the car forwards a little so that it was parked underneath the canopy of a tree. She dimmed the lights and pulled up the collar of her coat, tucking in her long hair. I stayed crouched in the backseat. I couldn't see what was going on around the station doors, nor could I check my watch. About fifteen minutes later, a woman suddenly opened the car door and hopped inside.

"Why didn't you tell me you were coming to pick me up?" the woman said to Yau Ying. It was Tou Lei. She quickly realized that the person sitting in the driver's seat was not Daihoi. It was incredibly awkward. I didn't know whether to sit up or remain crouching.

"I'm sorry!" Tou Lei said and started to open the car door.

"It's pouring outside. Why don't you let me drive you home?" Yau Ying stepped on the gas and we sped off.

"Who are you?" Tou Lei asked Yau Ying.

I sat up in the backseat, startling Tou Lei.

"What do you two want?" She was clearly frightened.

"Relax. We're not kidnapping you," Yau Ying said to her.

But Yau Ying sure was acting like a kidnapper. She had to be seriously crazy.

"I'm Daihoi's girlfriend," Yau Ying said.

Tou Lei grew silent. She seemed to no longer be frightened.

Yau Ying drove to a secluded area and stopped the car.

"How long has this been going on?" Yau Ying asked her.

"You should ask Daihoi."

"How far have you gone?" Yau Ying asked her.

Tou Lei let out a small chuckle. "What do you mean by 'how far have you gone'? We aren't children."

"Does he love you?"

I hadn't expected Yau Ying to ask that question.

"I wouldn't be with a man who didn't love me," Tou Lei said. "If I hurt you, I'm sorry."

"You're in no position to apologize to me!" Yau Ying said coldly. "Now get out of the car!"

"You said you'd drive me home."

"Don't even try it!" Yau Ying pushed her out, and Tou Lei fell into the gutter.

"You were blinded by rage just now," I said. "If she goes to the police, we're going to end up in prison."

Yau Ying was sobbing as she drove. I hadn't seen her cry since we were kids.

"Don't cry. You should listen to what Daihoi has to say. Maybe it's all a one-sided delusion on her part."

"I'm positive they've been sleeping together," Yau Ying said.

I didn't know what to say.

"Don't do anything stupid!" I told her when she dropped me off at home.

Yau Ying called me at four in the morning.

"Chow Jeoi, if you had to choose between happiness and stability, and you could only have one, which would you choose?"

"Stability can be a form of happiness," I said.

"You can only choose one."

"I've already chosen happiness. That's why my life is so unstable right now." I laughed darkly.

She was silent.

"Are you all right?" I asked her. "What did Daihoi say?"

"He admitted it. That woman had already called him before I got home and told him what happened."

"Are you going to leave him?"

"I don't know. It's been seven years. I thought he was going to be the man I'd marry."

"What did he say?"

"He asked me to marry him."

"Marry him?"

"I'm going to be happy, just like you." Yau Ying hung up.

I wasn't sure what she meant by that. Was that even an answer? If I had to choose between stability and happiness, and I could only choose one, I'd choose happiness, even though it was a kind of happiness that a person could get tired of.

The next day, in the early morning hours, I heard what sounded like someone knocking on my door. But it wasn't the door. There was someone at my window. Was it Sam? Could it be that he'd seen the puzzle in the window? I moved the puzzle and saw that Yau Ying was squatting on the escalator.

"You're not up yet, are you?" she asked me. "I picked up some breakfast."

Yau Ying came in through the main entrance. She'd bought deep-fried breadsticks, sticky rice, and soy milk.

"Did you give him an answer?" I asked.

"I said no."

"Why? All this time you wanted him to propose to you, didn't you?"

"I was hoping that we'd be together for the rest of our lives. He only proposed to me just now because he felt guilty."

"You can't forgive him?"

Yau Ying looked at me for a long time, then said, "No."

"Does he love that woman?"

"I don't know, but he doesn't love me anymore. He only asked me for the sake of doing the right thing. But as soon as we started making wedding plans, he'd regret it. We'd both hate each other. I don't need his charity."

"Don't you think it's a shame, though? Honestly, he's a good catch. You've been together for seven years. It doesn't seem worth it to let him get away for no good reason."

"The deed for our apartment is in both of our names. He promised he'd give me half."

"Would you accept it?"

"I can't think of any reason not to. I'm not as generous as you are. I've been deeply invested in this. For a woman, seven years isn't a short time. Since he's willingly and gladly giving it to me, why should I turn it down?"

"He's willing to give you the apartment because he feels guilty! Didn't you just say you didn't need his charity?"

"It's not charity. It's what I deserve. But marrying him is different. We'd have to spend the rest of our lives together. If I felt like I was getting charity all that time, that'd be painful."

"Why don't you give him another chance? This is the first time he's ever cheated."

Yau Ying set down her cup and said, "Some people like it when there's three competitors and only two winners. Me, I like a guaranteed victory."

"You're the strongest woman I know."

"Even though I'm only a 32A, I'm as staunch as a 36FF," Yau Ying said, laughing.

"Is Daihoi going to move out?"

"Yeah, he's going to look for a new place." Yau Ying stood up. "I have to go to work."

To my surprise, Daihoi came to see me the next day. He was usually immaculately dressed and coiffed, but when he showed up this time, his hair was slightly disheveled and he looked haggard. Yau Ying had appeared rational and detached by comparison.

"Did you find an apartment yet?" I asked him as we walked to a nearby café.

"I'm staying with Tou Lei for the time being."

"Yau Ying is deeply hurt."

"She's the one who wanted to break up."

"Men are so unwilling to take responsibility! You're the one who cheated. And now you're moving in with that woman?" I scolded him.

"I'm not getting love from anyone!" he told me dejectedly.

"You have two women, and yet you say that no one loves you?" I shook my head.

"I've never felt like Yau Ying loved me. Maybe she does, but she doesn't need me," Daihoi said.

The situation suddenly struck me as funny. It seemed as if Daihoi and Yau Ying had somehow switched roles. He'd become the woman, and she'd become the man. Usually it was women who needed to be told constantly that they were loved and needed.

"She loves you. She loves you a great deal, in fact," I said. "She needs you."

"She's never told me that before."

"Have you ever told her? You've never told her, either, have you?"

"The night before last, I told her, but she didn't believe me."

"It was too late," I said.

"Right. It was too late."

"How long has this been going on with this other woman?" I asked him.

"About a month!" He'd given up seven years of love for a month-long fling. I could understand why Yau Ying was so hurt—those seven years obviously meant nothing to him.

Daihoi moved out three days later. Those seven years of love took only three days to bring to an end.

Three weeks later, Yau Ying secretly went to the courthouse to hear the case he was working on. It was her way of saying good-bye.

The case was a personal dispute. A couple had been living together for fourteen years, and their relationship had fallen apart. They had bought an apartment together. The man had provided the down payment, but only the woman's name was on the deed. After they split up, the man wanted to sell the apartment for a profit, but the woman insisted that the apartment belonged to her. Their disagreement had escalated, and Daihoi was representing the man in the case.

Daihoi was completely unaware of the fact that Yau Ying was in the room, seated just a few rows behind him. Weeks earlier Daihoi had told her that his client had no chance of winning the case. Daihoi had already discussed the matter with the legal team for the opposing side, and they'd agreed to ask the two parties to settle the case out of court. But each appeared to be intent on destroying the other.

Yau Ying watched the man. He was wearing a suit and gold wire-frame glasses and looked rather intelligent. The woman had lovely features. They both looked highly educated. Yet they were headed into a duel to the death over $300,000.

There was only a handful of people in the courtroom, among them two court reporters taking endless notes.

When it was Daihoi's turn to take the floor, he stood up and said, "Your Honor, as the counsel for the plaintiff, I feel rather conflicted. This couple has lived together for fourteen years. They once loved each other deeply, and suddenly, they had a falling out. If money could be exchanged for fourteen years of love, I'm sure that most people would much rather have love. The fact that it's fourteen years makes no difference. Even half of fourteen years is a long time. For a person to throw away such a thing is a sad state of affairs indeed. I believe that the party who readily provided the down payment for a home to be jointly owned by the couple is the one who loved more deeply. But it seems that both my client and the defendant have failed to love deeply enough . . ."

For the first time since their breakup, Yau Ying shed a tear. For Daihoi to speak of half of fourteen years of love—the seven years that he and Yau Ying had been together—was more touching than anything he'd ever said before.

The judge ruled in favor of the plaintiff. The apartment was to be sold, and the profits were to be divided equally between the plaintiff and the defendant. Daihoi had won the case.

Yau Ying left the courtroom immediately after hearing the verdict. She didn't want Daihoi to know that she was there. When Daihoi first agreed to take on the case, Yau Ying had asked him what he'd do if the same thing happened to them. Laughing, Daihoi had told her, "That man's a fool. The deed had her name on it. Our deed has both of our names on it. Everyone gets 50 percent. If everyone gets half, there's no fighting."

Now he was leaving the apartment to her. He'd just said that the party who readily provided the down payment for a home to be jointly owned by the couple was the one who'd loved more deeply. If he really was the one who'd loved more deeply, why did he go out and get involved with another woman? Was it because the depth of that love wasn't mutual?

Yau Ying told me all of this when I was at her apartment that night.

"It's hard to tell if he left those clothes on purpose," I said, looking at a pile of clothes that Daihoi had left behind. "That way, he can come back anytime to pick them up."

"He's not going to. He's already handed in his letter of resignation," Yau Ying said.

"He's quitting his job?"

"Because I said I'm quitting, so he decided to quit first. We can't work together. I'd never be able to handle it."

"Daihoi said the party who readily provided the down payment for a home to be jointly owned was the one who loved more deeply. And now he's renouncing two things—this apartment and his job," I said.

"He's the one who stopped being faithful. Now it looks like I'm the one who's heartless."

"I sold the apartment and Sam still hasn't cashed the check. We both loved deeply." I lay on the bed contentedly.

Yau Ying stood up and said, "I wish I had the courage to renounce something."

Someone knocked on the door.

"It's not Daihoi, is it?" I asked.

Yau Ying went to answer it and found Chui Yuk and Yu Mogwo.

"I'm just dropping her off. I won't be taking part in this gathering you ladies are having," Yu Mogwo said.

"Why don't you have a seat—if you don't mind the scent of heartbreak, that is." Yau Ying poured two glasses of cold water.

"How are things going with your publishing house?" I asked Yu Mogwo.

"Great. We already bought the rights to a few Japanese manga titles. And it's all thanks to the money that you and Yau Ying lent us," Yu Mogwo said.

Chui Yuk winked at me.

"Yu Mogwo's new book is coming out next month," Chui Yuk said. "He wrote it in a week."

"That fast?"

"This book went a lot faster. In any case, I'm going to head out. I have to meet someone," Yu Mogwo said.

"Are you done shooting that video?" I asked Chui Yuk.

"We wrapped up yesterday." She let out a deep sigh.

"Congratulations," Yau Ying said.

I couldn't bring myself to congratulate her. When all was said and done, she'd sold her self-respect in order to help her man succeed.

"I found a job," Chui Yuk said.

"What kind of job?" I asked her.

"It's at a modeling agency. I'm going to handle recruitment. Since I haven't had a proper job these past few years, it's time for me to settle down. At the end of the day, modeling isn't a long-term gig."

"It seems like you've matured," I barely managed to say.

"I have! And it's all because of that video," Chui Yuk said.

"What do you mean?" Yau Ying asked.

"I suddenly felt old," Chui Yuk said with a pained laugh.

Though she didn't say it in so many words, the process of shooting that video had clearly taken a serious toll on her.

Yu Mogwo's latest novel, *The Magic Clock*, was well received. I saw quite a few people reading it on the train. Chui Yuk gave me a copy, and it was the first time I'd ever read an entire science-fiction novel from cover to cover. All of a sudden, Yu Mogwo became a huge success. His book went into multiple printings, and his previous books started to sell well as a result. He was interviewed by several magazines that recognized him as a singular talent among a new generation of science-fiction writers. Chui Yuk felt that it had been worth all the struggle.

Yu Mogwo invited Yau Ying and me to dinner at a Middle Eastern restaurant. He said he wanted to thank us since he would never have been able to start his publishing house or finish writing his book if we hadn't lent him the money.

But contrary to what I had expected, Yu Mogwo didn't look excited at all. Chui Yuk was the one who was excited.

"I've read this book ten times. It just keeps getting better every time," Chui Yuk said.

"I've recommended it to lots of my colleagues. They all say it's good. I'm helping you promote it!" Yau Ying quipped.

"When's the next one coming out?" I asked Yu Mogwo.

"I haven't decided what it's going to be about yet," Yu Mogwo said.

Clutching Yu Mogwo's hand, Chui Yuk told us, "There's a film production company that wants to make *The Magic Clock* into a movie!"

Yu Mogwo didn't even look terribly excited about that. Maybe he'd struggled for too long, and success wasn't going to change him overnight. Perhaps that was a good thing—at least he wouldn't cheat on Chui Yuk just because he got famous.

"I don't think it'll be long before I can pay you two back," Yu Mogwo said.

"Good! I look forwards to getting it back," I said, laughing.

Yau Ying chimed in. "Me, too!"

Chui Yuk cast a quick glance in my direction.

If the timing had been a little better, Yu Mogwo would've been able to finish writing *The Magic Clock* a little sooner, and Chui Yuk wouldn't have had to bare all. Even if they did have money now, they could never buy back that video.

***

A few days later, Yu Mogwo went to a friend's place, where he watched a video starring Chui Yuk. It finally dawned on him where the $300,000 had come from.

Chui Yuk denied that it was her, but she couldn't fool Yu Mogwo. He packed up his things and left. Chui Yuk bawled her eyes out. She called me and said she wanted to kill herself. I went over to see her right away.

"I'll go explain things to him," I said. "After all, you did it for him."

"He won't believe you," Chui Yuk said, sobbing.

"Where do you think he is? I'll go find him."

"I don't know."

I called Yau Ying and asked her to come over and take care of Chui Yuk. Then I went to the publishing firm's office to find Yu Mogwo.

The door was locked. I rang the buzzer. Inside, the lights were turned off. Just as I was about to leave, I heard a pager going off inside.

"Yu Mogwo, I know you're in there. Chui Yuk just threatened to kill herself. If you're a man, open the door. Now."

I was so angry that I kicked the door with all of my might.

"Yu Mogwo, come out!"

Yu Mogwo remained inside, cold and indifferent. Unable to restrain myself any longer, I shouted at the door. "You think that just because your girlfriend took off her clothes for a video, that you're the one who lost face, isn't that right? Why'd she even have to do it in the first place? Who'd she do it for? Isn't it because you needed $300,000 to start your publishing house? Do you know how humiliating it is for a woman to have to strip naked? If she didn't love you so much, she never would've been able to do it! But you, you're selfish to the bone. You only care about yourself. You just keep fantasizing while your poor girlfriend keeps picking up the tab to help you realize your precious little dreams . . ."

Yu Mogwo just ignored me, so I had no choice but to leave. I didn't know what I'd tell Chui Yuk, but I had to go back and explain.

Yau Ying opened the door for me.

"Did you find him?" she asked.

Chui Yuk looked at me expectantly, but I didn't know what to say.

"Well? Was he there?" Yau Ying questioned me.

I nodded.

"He won't forgive me. How many men do you know who could handle it if their girlfriends did something like this?" Chui Yuk sobbed.

"If he's not coming back, you shouldn't love him," Yau Ying said. "How many women would do something like that for their men?"

"Right. If he doesn't come back, then he's not worthy of your love," I said.

"I'm going to go see him." Chui Yuk stood up and went to the bathroom to wash her face.

"We're coming with you," Yau Ying said.

"You don't have to. It's my problem. I'll take care of it myself."

Chui Yuk took off alone and stood outside Yu Mogwo's office all night. Eventually, Yu Mogwo opened the door, and they embraced and cried.

That's what Chui Yuk told me. She happily described it as a test. It showed her just how deeply the two of them loved each other. But things weren't that simple. While their relationship was being put to the test, another test was on its way. Someone had stepped forward to denounce *The Magic Clock*, claiming that Yu Mogwo had plagiarized his own novel, and he was now seeking to halt further sales of the book.

"He didn't plagiarize anyone," said a worried Chui Yuk.

But this guy named Mak Kingtin had hired a lawyer to bring a copyright infringement suit against Yu Mogwo.

I didn't believe that Yu Mogwo would plagiarize someone else's work. But if it weren't true, why would this person be suing him?

Chui Yuk asked Yau Ying to help them find a lawyer, and Yau Ying recommended someone with experience in copyright-related matters. The legal fees weren't cheap, and sales of *The Magic Clock* had been halted. Where was Yu Mogwo going to get the money to hire a lawyer? Was Chui Yuk going to have to bare it all again?

"What did Yu Mogwo say?" I asked her.

"He said he didn't plagiarize it. He's so talented—why would he ever do such a thing?" said Chui Yuk, who was upset.

"Our lawyer, Mr. Wan, said the other side has proof. Mak Kingtin submitted his work to the newspaper where Yu Mogwo was working, and his novel is almost identical to Yu Mogwo's *The Magic Clock* except for a few parts," Yau Ying said.

"If he submitted his work last year, why would Yu Mogwo wait until now to plagiarize it? It doesn't make sense," Chui Yuk said.

"Mak Kingtin submitted the same book to a publisher in the newspaper group at the beginning of this year. They had no plans to publish it, but the manuscript was sitting there the whole time. They can prove it. In other words, Mak Kingtin's novel was there before Yu Mogwo's new book was released," Yau Ying said.

"Yau Ying, what are you saying? Are you really saying that Yu Mogwo is a plagiarist?" Chui Yuk was indignant.

"That's not what Yau Ying is saying." I was trying to be positive.

"What I'm trying to say is that Yu Mogwo might not necessarily win this lawsuit," Yau Ying said awkwardly.

"Then I'm getting a different lawyer! I'm sorry, but I have to go!" Chui Yuk stormed off.

"Why'd you have to say that?" I snapped at Yau Ying.

"Because if Yu Mogwo really did plagiarize Mak Kingtin, he's not likely to win the lawsuit. What's the point in wasting money on legal counsel, then? You and I both know that Chui Yuk is the one footing the bill," Yau Ying said.

I recalled the letter that Yu Mogwo had sent to Chui Yuk, in which he had written so eloquently about hummingbirds. He was talented. Why would he need to plagiarize?

That evening, I went to see Chui Yuk. I invited her out to dinner, but she didn't feel like going out.

"Where's Yu Mogwo?" I asked her.

"He went out."

"Don't be mad at Yau Ying," I said.

"That lawyer, Mr. Wan, shouldn't have told Yau Ying all of that! We're thinking of finding a different lawyer." Chui Yuk clearly wasn't ready to forgive Yau Ying.

"What did Yu Mogwo say?"

"He's in a bad place right now. Chow Jeoi, do you believe that Yu Mogwo would plagiarize someone else's work?"

I didn't know how to answer. I didn't think things were that simple.

"Even you don't believe him?" Chui Yuk was dismayed.

"I believe him." I didn't want to see Chui Yuk unhappy.

"No, only I believe him."

"What are you going to do if there's proof that Yu Mogwo did it?"

"I'm going to leave him," Chui Yuk said.

"It's not that serious, is it?"

"Unless he tells me the truth right now."

A drunken Yu Mogwo walked in just then.

"Why were you drinking?" Chui Yuk asked, rushing over to help him stand up.

I helped carry Yu Mogwo over to the sofa.

"He never drinks." Chui Yuk squatted down in front of Yu Mogwo and tenderly caressed his face.

"I'll go get a wet cloth," I said.

When I returned, Chui Yuk and Yu Mogwo were locked in a cozy embrace on the sofa. I put the cloth down on the coffee table and snuck out the door.

The next day, Chui Yuk called me and said, "He told me everything. Can you come meet me?"

She sounded distressed. Whatever she had to tell me, it didn't sound like good news.

After work, I met Chui Yuk at a café. It was a cold day, and I wanted a hot cup of coffee.

"I'm freezing to death." I took off my gloves.

The cold had turned the tip of Chui Yuk's nose bright red.

"He confessed. He plagiarized that other person's novel," Chui Yuk said despondently.

"Why'd he do it? He should've known that someone would find out sooner or later."

"He said he was under too much pressure. He didn't actually think anyone would find out."

"What are you going to do now?"

"That's his problem. I'm breaking up with him," Chui Yuk said firmly.

"You're going to leave him at a time like this?" I wouldn't ever have guessed that Chui Yuk would be the one to end the relationship.

"I said that if there was proof that Yu Mogwo plagiarized someone else's work, I'd leave him."

"You shouldn't force yourself to break up with him just because of that."

"No, I can die for him, I can sell my honor for him, but I can't accept the fact he's a swindler."

"You said that if he told you the truth, you'd forgive him."

"I've changed my mind."

"Don't you still love him?"

"I love him and I believe in him. I believe he's talented. It's because I wanted him to display his talents that I went out and made that video. This morning, I suddenly realized that it was all a big fraud. He can deceive whomever he wants, but he shouldn't have tried to deceive me."

Not long before, she had been standing at the door of the publishing house, waiting for Yu Mogwo to come out. She'd been completely unwilling to abandon him. The only explanation for her change of heart was that she'd worshipped Yu Mogwo a little too much, and her faith in him had come crashing down in one blow. She went straight from extreme love to extreme hate.

I agreed to go back to her place to help her pack up her things.

"Are you really moving out?" I asked her before we went inside.

Chui Yuk nodded. She took out the key and unlocked the door.

Inside, there was only a single lamp turned on. A listless, lethargic Yu Mogwo sat in the living room.

"I came to pack up my things," Chui Yuk said and went into the bedroom.

I stood there awkwardly. I didn't know whether to go help Chui Yuk or try to comfort Yu Mogwo.

"If you tell her not to go, she'll listen," I said to Yu Mogwo.

"It's no use," he said.

"How do you know if you haven't tried?"

Yu Mogwo looked up at me and said, "Isn't it crazy? I never thought anyone would find out. It's like all those Olympic athletes who take steroids—they never think they'll get caught. The only thing they care about is winning. I was working at the newspaper when the novel came in. I read it once through, and my hands started shaking. I kept thinking I could write something like it. At that point, I didn't have any plans to plagiarize it. I went to the States, came back, and wrote another book, but it wasn't good. Then, by chance, I opened the drawer and this novel was there. I thought no one would ever know . . ."

"That's the sort of thing you should never, ever do," I said.

"I was just too impatient. I wanted success—and this book was a success, no doubt about it. It was better than anything I could write. But I was also really unhappy. I didn't want it to be a success because its success would mean that I was a failure."

I finally understood why he hadn't been very excited about the success of the new book.

"If that book hadn't been a success, none of this ever would have happened." He smiled sardonically. "At least Chui Yuk wouldn't be leaving me."

"So you're just going to watch her go?"

"I'm the one who let her down. If I'd known how she earned that $300,000 I used to start the publishing house and put out this book, I never would've plagiarized someone else's work. I wouldn't forgive me if I were in her place." Yu Mogwo stood up.

"Where are you going?"

"I can't watch her leave," he said and walked out.

"Chow Jeoi, come help me," Chui Yuk called out from the bedroom.

Chui Yuk took a few articles of clothing and shoved them into a duffle bag.

"Where are you going?" I asked her.

"I'm going home, back to my family."

Chui Yuk placed her key on top of the coffee table.

"Are you sure about this?" I asked her.

"He's a swindler." Chui Yuk buried her head in my shoulder.

I patted her back.

"Let's leave before I change my mind," she said, picking up her luggage. Then she suddenly remembered something. "Hold on a second."

She went out to the balcony and removed from the laundry rack a pink lace bra that I'd bought for her. She put it in her bag.

I escorted Chui Yuk home. Her mother looked surprised to see her, though she'd gotten pretty good at acting nonchalant about these things. This wasn't the first time Chui Yuk had moved back home after living with a boyfriend. This time, she'd been away for a long while, and no one had expected her to come back.

"Please tell Yau Ying that I'm sorry," she said as she walked me out.

The temperature had dropped, and I was so cold as I waited for a taxi that my entire body was shaking and my nose wouldn't stop running. What was I doing without a man in this kind of weather? What a failure I was! If Sam were here to hold me, I'd be warm—I knew that much.

***

When I got home, I made myself a steaming hot cup of instant noodles. I took two bites before I realized that it tasted funny. It turned out that the package had expired six months ago.

I heard someone knocking at my window. Figuring it was Yau Ying again, I moved the puzzle aside. But standing there outside my window was none other than Sam. I didn't know whether to open the window or grab the puzzle and cover it up again. I watched him shivering in the cold wind. I couldn't bear to see him looking so cold. I opened the window.

"I was passing by, and I saw this puzzle. So you really do live here." His breath was as white as smoke as he spoke.

Day and night, I'd been praying that one day he'd randomly pass by and see the puzzle that he'd put together for me and know that I lived there, then knock on my window—and that was it. My wish had come true. I couldn't believe it. Still, I didn't know whether to invite him in.

"Can I come in?" he asked me.

There he was, trembling in the cold, asking me to let him in. I had imagined him holding me, and he'd really appeared.

"I'm on the second floor. Unit B," I told him.

I stood outside the door to my apartment, waiting for him.

"Come in and sit down," I said.

"So this is where you live? This place is a hovel."

It was as if he felt I'd suffered a great injustice.

"This is all I can afford," I said.

"It's freezing out there." He took my hands.

His hands were cold, so cold that they sent a chill straight to my heart.

"Let me make you a hot cup of tea." I broke free of his grip.

"Thank you," he said.

A long time had passed since either of us had uttered those two words—"thank you"—to one another. It seemed simultaneously natural and strange to say them now.

I poured him a cup of tea.

"What were you doing on this street?" I asked.

"I'd never taken this pedestrian escalator before. This evening I got a sudden urge to check it out. I never expected . . . what a coincidence. When I saw that puzzle, I thought I was dreaming."

"How have you been?" I asked.

"You're still wearing that necklace?" He pointed at the chain hanging around my neck.

"Let's not get into that!" I said, suddenly feeling flustered.

"You don't want me to be here, do you?" he said.

"I worked so hard to break free from you," I said.

"Was pain all I ever gave you?" he asked sadly.

"The person who gives you happiness is the same person who can give you pain."

He looked at me in silence.

"Why have you been so slow to cash that check?" I asked him.

He opened his wallet and took out the check that I had given him. "I carry this check with me everywhere, but I won't ever cash it. I wouldn't be able to live with myself if I did."

"I can go to the bank and give the money to you personally."

"I don't want it."

"If you don't want it, then I'll give that $2.8 million to your bank so that you can invest it all in the most high-risk currency for me," I said, wanting to spurn him.

"I'll help you make a profit from it," he said.

I was so mad at him that I burst out laughing. He grabbed my hand and said, "I miss you so much."

"Really?" I tried to look detached.

"Will you come back to me?" Sam put his arms around me. He wrapped his coat over my shoulders, and I felt incredibly warm.

"I don't want this." I pushed him away. "If I came back to you, what would happen? Wouldn't it be the same as before, with you sneaking around to see me? I'll only ever get half of you. Just let me go." I retreated to the edge of my bed.

Sam came over to my bed and pulled me down onto the bed with him. I wanted so badly to kiss him, but I wasn't about to go back to him that easily. I pressed my lips shut and firmly resisted the urge to respond. He started to fondle my breasts, but I pushed him away.

"I don't want this," I said, standing up.

He looked crushed.

"Can you leave?" I said cruelly.

"Do you still love me?" he asked me from the edge of the bed.

In my heart, I was crying. I was deliberately causing him pain. Why, at this point, did he not have the courage to get a divorce? All he had to do was promise me that he'd get a divorce, and I'd take him back in an instant. I wanted all of him. I'd accommodated him too much. He knew I'd stay with him even if he didn't divorce her.

I wanted to say no, but I couldn't bring myself to. Out of my desire for revenge, I didn't answer his question.

Dejectedly, he stood up from the bed.

Why wouldn't he just tell me he'd get divorced? Was he afraid to say those words? I wasn't going to tell him I loved him. Without a doubt, he'd be back the next day, and if not, then he'd be back the day after that. He knew that I lived here. He'd come back. I was just scared that when he did, I wouldn't know how to turn him away.

Unable to wait any longer for me to answer, he left without saying another word.

I threw myself onto the bed and bawled my eyes out. It was the first time he'd ever asked me if I loved him.

6

I'll Wait Forever for You

I thought about him all night.

The next day, I couldn't even force myself to concentrate on work. I missed him so much. He had passed by my window by sheer chance. That had been fate. Why was I lying to myself?

That afternoon, someone by the name of Ms. Lee called, claiming to be an employee of the Produce Green Foundation. "Am I speaking to Chow Jeoi? I'm calling to inform you that the calf that you adopted was born."

I had adopted a calf?

"I didn't adopt any calf," I told her.

"Do you know a Sam? He adopted the calf in your name."

The next morning, I boarded a train to go visit the Produce Green Foundation and see why Sam would adopt a calf for me. When I arrived at the farm, Ms. Lee took me on a tour. There were lots of cattle there, including the newborn, which happened to be nursing at that very moment.

"You can name him," she said.

"What on earth is this all about?" I asked.

"Mr. Tong didn't tell you? There are lots of cattle here in the New Territories. After they get older, no one wants them anymore, so they roam along the roads and often get hit by cars. So we buy them from the farmers and have city residents adopt them, so the cattle don't have to roam anymore. The response has been tremendous. There's a waiting list for adoptions. Last October, Mr. Tong came and signed up to adopt one. Since all our cattle were adopted, he asked to reserve the calf of a pregnant cow. He said it was a birthday present for his girlfriend and that he'd bring her to see the mother on November 3. But neither of you ever showed up. Afterwards Mr. Tong called us and asked us to get in touch with you when the calf was born."

So Sam had wanted to give me a calf for my birthday. No wonder he told me I had to see it. I felt a sudden tenderness towards the calf that was now nursing in front of me. I squatted down and rubbed its belly.

"There's also a plot of land that's yours." Ms. Lee pointed to a lot encircled with bamboo poles. "You can grow vegetables there."

"What's he giving me all of this for?"

"He said he wanted to give you a birthday present that was special. This plot is optimal for growing vegetables. Mr. Tong told me that you two wanted to open a French restaurant someday. Well, this will make it easy for you to grow your own produce, won't it?"

I named the calf Cherbourg.

When you love someone, you have to hate them a little. You hate them because they make it impossible for you to hate them. Sam was someone that I hated.

It was still freezing cold outside when I left the farm, but the sun was shining brightly and my heart was flooded with warmth. Sam had been thinking about our restaurant. On the train, I started trying to decide what kind of vegetables to grow on that piece of land. We could plant carrots. Even if our restaurant never actually materialized, we could still sell them to Kwok Seon for her carrot cakes.

By the time I got to the shop, it was 3:30 p.m. I missed Sam so much. I wasn't going to deny it anymore: I loved him, and someday he'd make me his wife. Even if I couldn't stand the wait, what did it matter? I wanted to tell him that I had an answer to his question. I always had, still did, and always would love him.

I gathered the courage to call him on his pager. Thirty minutes, one hour, then two hours passed. I called his pager three more times. He still didn't call me back. No one answered his work number.

Why wasn't he calling me back? Didn't he care about me anymore? He must have thought I didn't love him. It couldn't be. He wouldn't do that.

When I got home from work, I sat in front of the window and thought, maybe he'll suddenly appear. Outside the window, things had grown intensely quiet. It was already past 11:00 p.m. I called his pager once more, but he still didn't answer. I knew it wasn't something he'd do deliberately.

I didn't sleep a wink that night. The following morning, he still hadn't called me back. If his pager was broken, he would've called the service and had them look into it.

After work, I called his office and asked for him. A man answered the phone.

"I'd like to speak with Mr. Tong," I said.

"Him?" Judging by the sound of the man's voice, there seemed to be a problem. "May I ask who's calling?"

"This is Ms. Chow," I said.

"Ms. Chow? My name is Jeung Gaacung. I'm a colleague of Mr. Tong's. Can we schedule a time to meet in person?"

"What on earth is going on?' I sensed something strange. "Has something happened to him?"

"Why don't you come over and we'll talk? I'll be waiting for you in the company cafeteria downstairs. How soon can you be here?"

"I'll be there in five minutes." I locked up the shop and hurried to the cafeteria. A man waved to me.

"Are you Ms. Chow?" he asked.

I nodded.

"Have a seat," he said.

"What about Sam? What's happened?"

He hesitated before speaking.

"What on earth is going on?"

"Sam is dead."

I couldn't believe what I was hearing.

"Yesterday he came back from lunch and went back to work at usual. Around three, I saw him slumped over his desk. I thought he'd dozed off. Around four, I saw that he was still slumped over his desk. I went over and patted him on the back, and discovered he was unconscious. I immediately called for help, and an ambulance took him to the hospital. The doctor said he had coronary heart disease and that he'd had a heart attack. There were no warning signs. He was already dead by the time he got to the hospital."

"No! He asked you to lie to me. He's afraid of being involved with me! His wife put you up to this, didn't she? I know there's no way he'd ever have a heart attack!" I screamed.

"It was all very sudden."

"Impossible."

"I can't believe it, either. But I saw them take him away with my own eyes. When they were carrying him out, he had his pager on, and it wouldn't stop going off. The stress in this line of work is ridiculous. You have to call it quits by the time you're forty."

"I don't believe you!" I said.

"There's something about it in today's paper. Maybe you missed it."

"Which paper?"

He passed a copy of a newspaper to me. "I knew you wouldn't believe me."

In an inconspicuous section of the paper was a photo of a man on a stretcher being carried out of a building by paramedics. A senior executive from the bank's foreign exchange department had died at work. The name of the deceased was Sam.

I didn't shed a tear.

"Sam told me about you two. A while back, he told me that if anything ever happened, I should let you know. He was afraid you wouldn't find out. He was a good man." Jeung Gaacung was choked with emotion.

No tears would come out of me. How could he do this to me?

I'd seen him outside my window. He'd knocked on my window. There, in the freezing cold, he'd knocked on my window. That had only been the day before. When he left, I'd watched him pass by my window. He was walking, and he was alive.

"Ms. Chow, can I walk you out?" Jeung Gaacung asked.

"No thank you." I tried to stand up, but was so shaky I fell to my knees.

"Are you all right?" he asked as he helped me back up.

"I'm going home."

"Let me take you there."

"No."

I didn't know how to find my way back home.

"Here's my business card in case you need anything." Jeung Gaacung handed me his card. "Can I call a friend for you? Someone who can come get you?"

I shook my head.

Sam was dead. At death's door, his last words had been "Do you still love me?" He'd been expecting me to tell him that I loved him. But I had coldly refused to answer. I only wanted to get even with him. I wanted him to come find me again. I wanted him to say that he would get divorced for me. I thought there'd be other chances in the future, that he'd come for me again. I'd imagined there'd be a tomorrow and the day after tomorrow . . . But really, I'd only hurt myself. Why had I been so callous towards him? He died believing that I didn't love him anymore. How could I have been so cruel? Why didn't I ask him to stay the night? When they carried him out, his pager wouldn't stop going off. That was me. I'd been trying to page him. I'd never imagined that this was how things would end between us. He was just about to come back to me.

Late that night, the phone rang at my apartment. I picked up the receiver.

"Hello . . . who is this?"

There was no sound from the other end.

"Who is this?"

No answer.

"Who is this?" I kept asking.

I sensed that it was Sam, and that he was calling me from wherever he was.

"I love you."

I spoke the words that I'd never told him.

Whoever was on the other end hung up.

Was it a dream, or had Sam really called me from wherever he was?

I clutched the telephone, but it didn't ring again.

At daybreak, I called Jeung Gaacung.

"I want to see him," I said.

"That's going to be difficult. The corpse is at the funeral home."

It was the first time I'd heard someone use the word "corpse" to describe Sam. Within two short days, he'd become a corpse.

"I want to see him. He called me last night," I said.

"What?" He sounded stupefied.

"Please help me find a way," I begged.

"The funeral is on Wednesday."

"Where?"

"His wife will be there. It might not be appropriate for you to show up at the funeral home."

"I want to be there," I said.

"I see," Jeung Gaacung said. "I'll try to find a way for you to see him the day before the funeral."

On Tuesday morning, I called Jeung Gaacung.

"Did you have any luck making arrangements for me to see Sam?" I asked him.

"Meet me downstairs in front of the office at eight tonight, OK?" he said.

I was there at 7:00. Jeung Gaacung came out at 8:00.

"Let's go find a place to sit down and talk," he said.

"Why? Don't we have to go?"

He was silent.

"There's no way for you to get me around his wife, is that it?"

"I'm sorry. Sam's funeral was yesterday."

"You said it was tomorrow!"

"It was suddenly moved forward."

"Why didn't you tell me?"

"Sam's wife never left the funeral home. His relatives were there, too. You wouldn't have been welcome."

"So you deliberately lied to me! I never should have trusted you!"

I'd never felt so helpless. I didn't even have the right to see him one last time, and I was the woman he'd been sleeping with for the past five years!

"Why did you have to lie to me?"

I yanked Jeung Gaacung's coat. I hated him.

"Ms. Chow, I just didn't want you to feel bad about it. That's what Sam would have wanted, isn't it? Everyone has to die. It makes no difference whether you see him or not. If there had been a scene at the funeral home, Sam wouldn't be able to leave this world in peace, would he?"

"Where is his grave? Please tell me."

"He was cremated," he said.

"Cremated? Why?" They hadn't left me even a corpse. "What about the remains? What about his remains?"

"They're at his home," Jeung Gaacung said.

At his home? He'd vanished in a puff of smoke, without allowing me even a glimpse of him.

"I'm sorry," Jeung Gaacung said.

I shouldn't have listened to him. I never should have trusted him. If Sam were here to see me being mistreated like this, he'd have stepped in and rescued me. I was certain of it.

I went back to my old apartment.

Kwok Seon opened the door.

"Ms. Chow? Is everything all right? You don't look so well."

"Can I come in?"

"Of course."

As I stepped inside the apartment, I saw that it was still decorated the way it had been before. The bed Sam and I used to sleep in was still there, and I went over and climbed onto the side where he had always slept, trying to soak up whatever was left of his warmth.

"Will you sell this apartment back to me? I want to live here," I said.

"What . . . ?"

"How much do you want? I can give you a better price than you paid. Please, I'm begging you!"

"Why would you want to do such a thing?"

"I regret selling it."

"If that's what you really want, no problem."

"Really?"

"I imagine that you must have a reason."

"I'll go get the money tomorrow. Can I sleep here tonight?"

"Of course. It's only me here anyhow."

The following day, I went to the bank and discovered that my account had been drained. What had happened to that $2.8 million? Had Sam cashed that check? The teller told me that the check had been cashed the day before.

Sam couldn't have cashed the check since he was dead. So who had deposited the money into his account? I couldn't think of anyone except his wife.

I called Kwok Seon and told her that I couldn't buy the apartment back.

I'd lost everything except that plot of land and that calf, Cherbourg.

I went to the farm to check on Cherbourg.

"Have you decided what kind of vegetables you're going to grow?" Ms. Lee asked.

I shook my head.

"You have to sow the seeds in spring," she said.

Spring? Spring seemed so far away. I put my arms around Cherbourg. He was born the night before Sam died. Sam had given him to me when he was still in his mother's womb, and by the time Cherbourg arrived in this world, Sam had already vanished.

I pulled Cherbourg into a tight embrace. He was the life that Sam had left behind for me. He was alive, newly arrived in this world.

For my birthday, Sam had given me a gift that was alive. Why did life and death have to go hand in hand like that?

My pager went off, frightening Cherbourg. I let go of him and called Yau Ying back.

"What's going on? You haven't been at work the past few days, and you haven't been at home, either, and when I call your pager, you don't call me back. I thought you'd gone missing. We're worried about you," Yau Ying said.

"Sam died," I said.

"What do you mean, he died?"

"He's already cremated. I didn't even get to see him one last time."

"Where are you right now?"

"Hok Tau Reservoir."

"Where's that? Don't move. I'm coming to get you."

I sat down on the edge of the pasture, holding Cherbourg in my lap and watching the sky darken. Eventually, I saw two familiar silhouettes coming towards me.

"This place was hard to find," Chui Yuk said.

"How did Sam die?" Yau Ying asked.

I leaned my head on her shoulder.

I hated Sam. He'd said he'd never leave me, but he'd lied. Even now, I still couldn't bring myself to shed a tear. He'd lied to me.

Two weeks later, I went back to work at the shop. Jenny and Anna didn't know what had happened or why I'd been away, and they didn't dare ask.

Chui Yuk and Yau Ying cried much more than I did, while I couldn't squeeze out so much as a single teardrop. Yau Ying suggested that the three of us should all go away on vacation together, but I didn't want to go anywhere. Although they were disappointed, I didn't want to leave the place where his remains were.

When it was nearly closing time, a woman came into the store. She was a little on the heavy side and about thirty-seven or thirty-eight years old. She wore a black dress and a long black coat. Her makeup was elegant, but even her pale foundation couldn't conceal the haggard face underneath.

"Feel free to have a look around, ma'am," I told her.

She picked out a black lace bra.

"Would you like to try that on?" I asked her.

"Are you the manager of this store?" she asked.

"Yes. I'm Ms. Chow."

"I'll try this one on."

"What size?" I asked her.

"This one should be fine."

"The fitting rooms are over here," I said, leading her to a room.

"You two can head out," I said to Jenny and Anna.

"Ma'am, how is that bra working out for you?" I asked her from outside the fitting room.

"Can you come in here and help me?" she asked me.

I stepped into the dressing room. She was fully dressed. She hadn't even tried on the bra.

"I'm Sam's wife," she told me.

I wanted to make a quick escape, but she shut the door and stood in front of it, blocking the exit.

"So you're my husband's mistress?" She stared at me.

I looked right back at her. If Sam were still alive, I might've been scared to confront her. But Sam had died, and I had nothing to be afraid of anymore.

This was the woman who wouldn't give me a chance to see Sam one last time. She disgusted me.

"You're the woman Sam was having an affair with all along. And you're none other than a seller of bras." She laughed contemptuously.

I had no intention of getting into a catfight with her.

"That idiot Sam thought he could have a little fun with another woman, nothing more. Then he suddenly decided to buy you an apartment worth more than $2 million." She shook her head and sighed.

How did she know about the money?

"You think I didn't notice that $2 million was missing from his bank account? I've known for a long time."

"What do you want?" I asked her.

"Fortunately, I discovered the check that you wrote him in his wallet. I'll have you know that I was the one who cashed it. That money used to be his. Now it's mine."

I'd suspected it was her, so this came as no surprise.

"Do you know why he was cremated?" she asked. "Because I didn't want him to have a grave. Cremated remains are supposed to be stored at a temple. I don't care who objects—I brought them home. It wasn't because I couldn't stand to be separated from him. Do you want to know why I did it?" She walked straight up to me, until she was practically touching me, then looked me in the eye and said, "I didn't want to give you an opportunity to pray for him. He was my husband, and even in death, he's still mine."

She let out a mean laugh.

"You're so cruel," I said.

"Cruel?" She cackled. "Who's been cruel to whom here? He still belongs to me."

"Is that what you think?"

The next thing I knew, she'd stripped off her coat and dress. She stood before me, almost naked, wearing only her black bra and panties.

Her breasts were small, her arms and belly were flabby, and her thighs were thick. It certainly wasn't the figure that I'd always imagined Sam's wife would have.

"I can't compete with you, is that right?" she asked.

I didn't reply.

"Because of you, Sam wanted to divorce me. He and I were together for almost eighteen years. We were each other's first love. He used to love me. Then he stopped loving me, and it's all because of you!"

She yanked open my jacket.

"What do you think you're doing?" I cried, grabbing her hand.

"Take off your clothes. Take them all off, and I'll give you back your $2.8 million." She tugged at my jacket. "I want to see what Sam was so attracted to. Take it off!"

I removed my shirt and skirt, until I was only in my white bra and panties. I stood directly before her.

She looked at my chest and didn't say a word. I already had her beaten.

"My husband was only attracted to your body. He needed to get it out of his system, that's all. He was like all men."

"If he'd just needed to get it out of his system, he wouldn't have been with me for five years. He used to love you, but on his deathbed, he loved me. The day before he died, he asked me whether I loved him," I told her.

She started to laugh. "It's too bad he made a mistake. You took off your clothes in front of me for $2.8 million—you only wanted his money! Well, I'll give you your check now. Think of it as your paycheck for sleeping with my husband for the last five years."

"I have no intention of accepting that money. That's my way of punishing you for not letting me pray for Sam." I put my clothes back on. "If he could somehow come back to life, I'd just as well give him to you. When you love someone, you don't try to control them. He was a good man to the core. Unfortunately, he's never coming back."

She let out a sharp cry and crumpled to the ground, sobbing. Her entire body was shaking, and my heart quickly softened. I took her coat and draped it over her.

She was a victim, too.

I left the fitting room. I had no idea how I managed to find the inner strength to cope with everything that had happened. If Sam and I had still been together, I never would have been able to hold it together. But he wasn't here, and no one was ever going to protect me the way he had. I knew I had to be strong.

Sam's wife exited the fitting room fully clothed and left the shop without so much as turning her head. I watched her disappear down the corridor of the shopping center.

I went back into the fitting room and kneeled down to pick up the bra that she'd left. My heart ached, and my limbs were so sore that I could barely move. I could no longer hold back the onslaught of tears. I hadn't had a good cry since Sam had gone. I had always thought that people cried when they were hurting the most, but in fact it was when you were hurting the most that you couldn't cry at all.

His departure had been too sudden. My pain turned into hate. I hated him for leaving me. I told myself that maybe if he hadn't loved me so much, he wouldn't have caused me so much pain. But today, his wife had told me that he'd brought up the subject of divorce. He'd been thinking about how the two of us could be together—maybe even spend the rest of our lives together—and I'd just never believed him. I had always thought he was just trying to buy himself time, that he lacked the courage to get a divorce. I'd misunderstood him. He had been willing to pay a huge price in order to be with me. If there were a way to bring him back, I'd rather have him just be alive and not love me that much.

I bawled loudly for a long time. Could he hear me? Could he hear me repenting over my refusal to answer his question? I shouldn't have treated his wife the way I just did. I should've asked her to let me see his remains. He'd once joked that his wife might turn him into minced meat sauce, but she'd just as easily turned him into cremated ashes. His love for me had already turned to dust, only to be found in that world between heaven and earth.

Every Sunday, I went to Hok Tau Reservoir to visit Cherbourg. He'd grown a lot, and he wasn't nursing anymore. I thought he recognized me.

One Sunday, Yau Ying and Chui Yuk went with me to see him.

"Daihoi came back," Yau Ying said to me.

"Did he really?" I was happy for her.

"He came back last night. He said there were some clothes that he hadn't taken when he moved out. Then he hung around and didn't leave."

"How could he possibly hang around and not leave, unless you wanted him to?" Chui Yuk teased.

"What'd he have to say?"

"He didn't have anything to say to me. But I had something to say to him."

"What did you have to say?"

"I told him that I loved him," Yau Ying said, blushing.

"You did? You really uttered those words?" I couldn't believe it.

"I love him. Why should I hide it?"

"So, was Daihoi moved?" I asked.

"That's why he didn't leave," Yau Ying said.

"It's over with Tou Lei, then?" Chui Yuk asked.

"He said it's over. I'm actually to blame, too. I'd never once tried to understand his inner world. I thought I knew him all this time, but I didn't. He loved me more than I loved him. If it weren't for what happened to Sam, I might not have had the guts to tell Daihoi that I love him. But if you love someone, you should let them know. If you don't, there'll come a day when you lose him forever."

"Very true," I said.

"Sorry. I didn't mean to bring that up," Yau Ying said.

"It's OK. I only have myself to blame. We were given five years together, but it was too short of a time. I'd gladly have spent a lifetime with him."

"If I had such a good man, I would, too," Chui Yuk said.

"You have to take good care of yourself—for him," Yau Ying said.

"I can do that," I said. "He'll protect me."

"Does this mean you'll give Chen Dingleung a second chance?" Chui Yuk asked.

"I haven't seen Chen Dingleung in ages. He's never been my backup choice," I said.

Chen Dingleung could never replace Sam. No man could ever take Sam's place.

The following afternoon, I ran into Chen Dingleung at a liquor store in Central.

"Chow Jeoi, I haven't seen you in ages," he said.

"What a coincidence running into you here," I said.

"The chance of us running into each other is higher than one in three hundred sixty-five. It doesn't seem so unusual at all!" He still hadn't forgotten about that one in three hundred sixty-five chance.

"Ah, right," I said.

"I heard about what happened. I'm sorry."

"Did Chui Yuk tell you?"

He nodded.

"I really loved him," I said.

"I could see that. Every one of us has been tormented by love at some point."

He noticed that I was holding a bottle of 1990 vintage red wine.

"You're having red wine, too?" he asked.

"I like red wine from 1990. That's the year he and I met," I said.

Ever since Sam died, I'd been buying wine from that year. That day I was buying three bottles.

"Well, 1990 is a good vintage," he said. "Wines from that year are worth preserving. That's what the books say."

"I'm lucky, then," I said.

I'd amassed eleven bottles of French red wine from that year. Chen Dingleung was right. The grape harvests from 1990 were good. Red wines from that year were constantly increasing in value. In fact, the prices had risen so quickly that I could now only afford a bottle a month.

The previous spring, I'd planted tomatoes in the plot of land that Sam gave me. Now Cherbourg was plowing the field. He was a year old, and he was healthy and strong. Big, red tomatoes were starting to appear in the field, and I gave lots of them away to Chui Yuk and Yau Ying. The tomatoes that I'd grown seemed to taste especially good. Daihoi and Yau Ying wanted to get a plot of their own.

One day a few months later, I met up with Chui Yuk. She said she had something she wanted to give me.

"What is it?"

"Open it up and see," she said, handing me a paper bag.

Inside was a shadow box that contained something that sort of resembled a honeybee, but not exactly. It had feet and two iridescent wings that gleamed like gemstones.

"It's a hummingbird. You said you wanted one, didn't you?"

That was a long time ago.

"Where'd you get this?"

"Yu Mogwo gave it to me."

"Are you two back together?"

"We're not getting back together, but we see each other every once in a while."

I examined the taxidermic specimen for a long time. It was the only thing that could fly backwards. It'd be nice to be able to travel backwards into the past. I'd be able to hold Sam in my arms again; we'd be keeping each other warm. Our love was a lot like a hummingbird: it was singular in this world.

I took the hummingbird home with me and bought a twelfth bottle of red wine from 1990. That day was the coldest yet of the beginning of winter. I wrapped myself in a blanket and put on "I Will Wait for You," which I hadn't listened to since Sam died.

Tap-tap-tap-tap. Someone was knocking at my window. I moved the picture away from the window. But no one was there. I opened the window, letting in a bone-chilling wind, but no one was outside. I recalled how Sam always told me, "I'll never leave you." It was on a freezing cold night like this that I saw him outside my window, and it was for the last time.

ABOUT THE AUTHOR

Photo © 2013 Amy Cheung

Amy Cheung is one of Hong Kong's most popular writers, well known throughout the Chinese-speaking world. Her first novel, *Women on the Breadfruit Tree*, appeared in serialized form in the daily newspaper *Ming Pao*. She has written more than forty widely acclaimed books, including novels and essay collections.